"We have the night. One night, Drea. Here. You and me."

"There is no you and me."

"There could be."

"Mason, we can't do this. There are things you don't know. Things that make this impossible."

"All I see are possibilities tonight."

He was pleading his case. It was hard saying no to him. Not when her body cried out for him. To know Mason that way once. Would that be a punishable crime?

She pivoted around slowly and Mason was there, in front of her, his eyes raking her in as if he'd already touched her. As if he was making love to her with his deep, dark gaze.

Just once.

Maybe she needed to finish this.

Yet she hated him more because she wanted him.

* * *

Texan for the Taking is part of the Boone Brothers of Texas series.

Dear Reader,

Welcome to Boone Springs, Texas! Here you'll meet all three of the Boone brothers: Mason, Risk and Lucas. Each one of these hunky guys has their own story of love, loss, redemption and inspiration.

We start off with widower Mason Boone, who lives on Rising Springs Ranch and runs the megacompany Boone Incorporated. In this ranching town his ancestors founded, Mason butts heads with his onetime family friend, Andrea "Drea" MacDonald, a woman who blames him for the destruction of her father's ranching business. A woman who has secrets and a more personal reason to fight off any attraction she has for Mason.

My inspiration in creating Boone Springs and the widespread ranching community came from visiting our Texas family members in towns very similar to Boone Springs. These proud, dedicated and hardworking people are also fun and free-spirited, as you'll witness in Mason and Drea.

I hope you enjoy all three of these tall Texas tales of love!

Until next time, happy reading!

Charlene

CHARLENE SANDS

——

TEXAN FOR THE TAKING

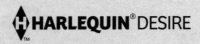

Recycling programs
for this product may
not exist in your area.

ISBN-13: 978-1-335-60363-0

Texan for the Taking

Printed in U.S.A.

www.Harlequin.com

Charlene Sands is a *USA TODAY* bestselling author of more than forty romance novels. She writes sensual contemporary romances and stories of the Old West. When not writing, Charlene enjoys sunny Pacific beaches, great coffee, reading books from her favorite authors and spending time with her family. You can find her on Facebook and Twitter, write her at PO Box 4883, West Hills, CA 91308, or sign up for her newsletter for fun blogs and ongoing contests at charlenesands.com.

Books by Charlene Sands

Harlequin Desire

The Slades of Sunset Ranch

Sunset Surrender
Sunset Seduction
The Secret Heir of Sunset Ranch
Redeeming the CEO Cowboy

Heart of Stone

The Texan's Wedding Escape
Heart of a Texan

Boone Brothers of Texas

Texan for the Taking

Visit her Author Profile page at Harlequin.com, or charlenesands.com, for more titles.

You can find Charlene Sands on Facebook, along with other Harlequin Desire authors, at Facebook.com/harlequindesireauthors!

To my sister, Carol, and her hubby, Bill,
two of the nicest people on earth.
Thanks for your love and support and
always being there for us!

And to Eric, Whitney, Reese and Quinn,
and Angi and Zane, my nieces and nephews
who make our family even more special!

One

Of course *he* had to be here.

Mason Boone.

Drea MacDonald had avoided him all these years, but there was no hope for it now. She had to deal with him on a strictly professional level. She liked to think she'd moved beyond what had happened, had moved way beyond *him*, but how could that be? Something that profound in her life, something that had scarred her so permanently, wasn't easily forgotten.

Mason pressed his tall frame against the back wall of the hospital conference room, arms folded, watching her through intense coal-black eyes. She couldn't ignore him. He was a presence in the room; a tall, dreadfully handsome man, dressed impeccably in a dark suit, who commanded respect and exuded confidence.

As a young girl, all those traits had lured her in. But he'd rejected her without a second thought.

Her best bet would be to treat him with indifference, to give him a nod and get on with her business. He didn't have to know the pain he'd caused her. He didn't have to see the hurt look in her eyes or the flush of her skin. It would take an award-winning performance, but she was up to the task. After all, she'd imagined this moment in her head fifty times, if not more.

Her heart sat heavy in her chest because she wasn't the only one who had lost something precious. She wasn't the only one who'd been deeply scarred. Mason had, too. He'd lost his wife and unborn child nearly two years ago. His loss and grief only contributed to the tremendous guilt she felt for disliking him so. He had the town's support. Everyone was sympathetic to his loss. It was hard to hate a guy everyone else rallied around. Guilt ate away at her even though she had every right to hold a grudge.

She stood at the head of the conference table, just finishing up her presentation. "And thanks to the generosity of Mason Boone and his family," she said, grinding her teeth as she gave him praise, "we'll hold our multifaceted weekend fund-raiser at Rising Springs Ranch. Our goal, two million dollars."

The doctors, hospital administrators and committee members overseeing the fund-raiser gazed at each other, raising skeptical brows. It was a tall order, true, but she had always banked her reputation on fulfilling her goals. And this part of Texas was rich with donors of cold hard cash.

"It's doable," said an assured voice from the back of the room.

All heads swiveled to Mason Boone. His family had founded the Texas town of Boone Springs decades ago, and the hospital had recently changed names from County Memorial to Boone County Memorial. The Boone family and their kin practically owned the entire town. Well, they owned the best parts, so when a Boone spoke, people listened.

"It's very doable, if we're smart," Drea persisted, again avoiding Mason's dark eyes. "And I intend to be…very smart."

"Thatta girl," gray-haired Dr. Keystone said. "We trust you, Andrea. You're one of our own."

"Thank you, Doctor. I appreciate your support. Together, we'll make this work."

She smiled, feeling powerful in her black suit and three-inch cherry-red heels. She wore her long, dark cocoa hair up in a sleek, practical style. She meant business.

Landing this job at the hospital served many purposes. Nailing it would all but guarantee her promotion to vice president at Solutions Inc., the consulting and events planning firm she worked for in New York. But more importantly, she wanted to help the community where she'd grown up by raising funds for a much-needed cardiac wing, to honor her mother, who'd died of heart failure. And she also wanted to reconnect with her ailing father. Unfortunately, that meant living in the cottage the Boones had gifted Drew MacDonald after practically stealing Thundering Hills Ranch out from under him. Her father's acceptance of the living arrangements irritated her to this day. How could he be okay with their charity, while Drea's life had been snatched right out from under her as a young girl when the Boones took over Thundering Hills? She'd lost her home, too, but her father hadn't seemed to notice how much that had disrupted her life.

After the meeting, as Drea collected her papers, carefully placing them in her briefcase, she heard footsteps approaching and held her breath.

"Nice job, Drea."

That deep confident voice unsettled her. The timbre, the tone, the way Mason said her name—memories came rushing back, tilting her world upside down. *God.* Why was he heading this committee? Deep in her belly, she knew. He'd lost his pregnant wife to heart disease. Drea couldn't really fault him for wanting to be involved; she had similar reasons for being here. Yet, even knowing the pain he'd recently endured, seeing him in the flesh for the first time in years curdled her stomach. She resented the Boones, but him most of all.

Mason stood facing her, his eyes boring in, and finally, because she felt defiant and fearless, she stared back and gave him her best aloof smile. "Thank you."

Twelve years had only given his good looks a more rugged edge. She took in the sharp angle of his jaw, the facial scruff that hadn't been there before, the length of his hair, whipped back and shining like black ink. None of it mattered. She was merely observing. She'd turned off all her buttons, leaving him none to push anymore.

"You look good," he said.

The compliment slid off her back.

"Drew will be glad to have you home."

"It's temporary," she said, closing the clasp on her briefcase.

"Still, it'll be good for him."

She looked away. What about what was good for her? What about all those days and nights when she'd had to be the adult because her father was passed out drunk on the floor? What about the dinners he'd never cooked, the clothes he'd never washed? What about a twelve-year-old kid having to baby her own father? And what about the heartsick motherless girl who'd desperately needed…love?

"We'll see."

"You haven't been home yet?"

She shook her head. "No, I came here straight from the airport."

"Drea?"

She couldn't look at him, even though there was something pleading in the way he'd said her name. Instead, she continued fiddling with the closure on her case.

"It's good to have you home," he said finally.

Chin down, she nodded. "I have a job to do."

"Yeah, about that. We should probably coordinate on the events you have planned. We could look at them over dinner one night or—"

"No." Her voice was sharper than she'd intended.

So much for being professional. He was staring at her like she'd lost her mind. Maybe she had, thinking she could come home in hopes of doing something good for the community, something to honor her deceased mother, even if it meant working alongside Mason. Were her emotions so tangled up that she couldn't separate her professional life from her private one?

Goodness, but she had to. She'd committed to this fund-raising campaign. She was being paid to see it through. And she had to remind herself over and over that she was doing this to honor her mother. It was time she came home. At least temporarily.

"No?" Mason narrowed his eyes.

"I mean, I'll email you. I really am very busy, Mason. I have a lot on my mind today."

She gave him a plastic smile, one he immediately picked up on as bullshit. He nodded. "Yeah, I get it." His mouth curled in a frown and there was an edge of annoyance in his voice now. *Ha!* He had no right being annoyed with her. Not when the last time she'd been with him, he'd treated her like dirt.

He slipped a business card into her hand, his long lean fingers skimming over her knuckles. Immediately her heart beat faster, her nerves jumped. The shock of his brief, warm touch strummed through her body. "Email me when you find time. We have exactly one month to pull this off."

His urgency wasn't lost on her. This was as important to him as it was to her. They had that in common. Both wanted a special cardiac wing of the hospital built in Boone Springs. But all of a sudden one month in Texas seemed like an eternity.

Not to mention she'd be living at the cottage on Rising Springs Ranch again.

On Mason's home turf.

"Yum, this is just as delish as I remembered." Drea swallowed a big hunk of her Chocolate Explosion cupcake. Unladylike, but Katie Rodgers, her bestie from childhood and owner of the bakery, would expect no less.

Her friend laughed and removed her apron. She put the Katie's Kupcakes is Klosed sign on the door and joined Drea at the café table.

"You do not disappoint," Drea said. "And you remembered my favorite."

"Of course I did. Can't forget all those times you'd come over and we'd bake up a batch. We were what, ten at the time?"

"Yeah, but ours never came close to these marvels you crank out at four in the morning. Gosh, you always knew what you wanted to do with your life. I'm so proud of everything you've accomplished, Katie. I bet you've got all of Boone Springs wrapped around your sugary fingers, with lines out the door in the morning."

"I have no complaints," she replied. "Business is good." She sighed sweetly. "It's great to have you back in town. I've missed you."

Drea grabbed Katie's hand and squeezed. "I've

missed you, too. I couldn't drive out to Rising Springs without seeing you first."

"I'm glad you did. Only I wish it wasn't temporary. I kinda like seeing you in person instead of on Facetime."

"Well, let's try to make the most of my stay here. We're gonna both be busy, but we have to make a pact to see each other a few times a week," Drea said.

"Pinkie promise?" Katie curled her last digit, and they linked fingers just like they had when they were kids.

"Pinkie promise."

"Good, then it's settled." Katie began to rise. "Would you like a cup of coffee to wash down the cupcake? I could brew up a fresh pot."

"When did your cupcakes ever need washing down?" She smiled. "No thanks. Any more coffee today and I swear I'll float away. Let's just talk."

Katie smiled and plunked back into her seat. "Okay. So, you're working on the hospital fund-raiser."

She nodded.

"With Mason?"

"Yeah, which is the major drawback to my coming home. I have to make the fund-raiser my high priority, so I'm enduring the Boones for as long as it takes."

"I get that it's hard for you, Drea. I really do. It was hard on Mason, too, losing Larissa and the baby. From what I hear, he's only just starting to come out of his grief."

"It's a tragedy. But let's not talk about the Boones.

Because if we do, then I'll have to ask you about Lucas."

Katie's eyes rounded. "Lucas? We're just friends. If that anymore."

"Uh-huh. So you say."

"For heaven's sake, he was engaged to my sister. And he broke Shelly's heart when he went off and joined the Marines."

"But I hear he's back now." Drea took another bite of cupcake, certain she'd die from an overdose of decadence.

"Don't remind me. Shelly still hasn't healed from him running out on her like that. It was such a shock. Luke seemed true blue. After the breakup, Shelly hit some rough patches. Mom's convinced it's all Luke's fault. I mean, it sounded more like something Risk would do. Not Luke."

River "Risk" Boone, heartthrob and one-time famous rodeo rider, was the player in the Boone family.

"Yeah, well, we can't forget he's a Boone. It's part of his DNA," Drea said.

Katie's right brow rose and she shook her head. "So, after all these years you haven't gotten over it, either?"

"Over what? The fact that the Boones preyed on my father's grief and then stole Thundering Hills out from under him? Our families had been friends for years, but as soon as my dad hit a rough patch, the Boones swooped in, stole our ranch and we were reduced to living at the cottage on Boone property. They gave Dad a pity job as caretaker. Then there's

Mason and all that he put me through… Oh, never mind. I don't want to rehash it." She waved her hand, ending her rant.

Katie gave her a serious knowing look. But Katie didn't know everything. Drea hadn't told her best friend what had happened after her debacle with Mason. How she ran into the arms of the first willing man and gave up her virginity. How she'd gotten pregnant and lost her baby. It had been the worst time of her life.

"I guess we need to put the past behind us, Drea. That's what I keep telling my sister."

"Yeah, easier said than done sometimes."

She was through talking about the Boones. She polished off the cupcake and licked the frosting from her fingers, closing her eyes as she relished every last morsel of goodness. "Mmm."

"So, I hear your dad is struggling a bit. The fall he took last week was pretty bad. When I heard about it, I stopped by his place with a batch of apricot thumbprints and half a dozen cupcakes."

"Ahh, you're the best. He loves your thumbprint cookies. Thanks for checking in on him."

"He's very excited to have you home."

"I know." She couldn't say too much; her emotions were curled up in a knot about going home to Drew MacDonald. Maybe that's why she was procrastinating. She'd missed her father, and she loved him. But she was a realist. Her dad would never win a Father of the Year award. Hard fact, but true.

"He's changed, Drea. He's trying very hard."

She sighed. "I'll believe it when I see it." She glanced at her watch. "Which is what I should do just about now. I hate to go, but I've really gotta get on the road."

"Will you text me later?"

"Of course."

They both stood and then Katie went behind the counter. "Just a sec. I'm not sending you home empty-handed." She packed up a white box with goodies and sealed it with a pastel pink Katie's Kupcakes sticker. "Here you go," she said, handing over the box. "Welcome home."

"Thanks, friend. My hips will never be the same."

"Your hips and my thighs. We're all doomed."

Drea chuckled and kissed Katie on the cheek. "At least we'll both go down together."

After she excited the shop, a sense of real doom flashed through her system.

She couldn't procrastinate any longer.

It was time to go to the place she'd never considered home.

Drea parked her car in front of her father's house just as the autumn sun was setting. Splashes of deep pink and purple painted the sky overhead. She'd forgotten the stunning sunsets in this part of Texas. How many years had it been since she'd seen a horizon so rich and vibrant? These wide-open spaces were tailor-made for such amazing spectacles. Texas was known for doing things large and the sight brought a little peace to her jittery heart.

Lordy be.

She chuckled at the slang that had come back to her after crossing state lines.

But she wasn't that Texas girl any longer.

She gazed toward the cornflower-blue cottage trimmed in white, and saw her father sitting in a rocking chair on the front deck. As soon as he spotted her, he made an attempt to rise. His face turned a shade of red, not from pain, she assumed, but from frustration as he faltered and slid back down onto the seat. On his next try, he pulled himself up and leaned against a post. His hair was lighter gray than she remembered, his body chunkier, but he was still a handsome man, and there was a spark in his green eyes as he waved to her.

She waved back, holding her breath. She reminded herself this wasn't the same drunken man who'd given up on life after her mother died. He was trying to be a good father. He'd honed his skills on a smartphone so he could send her text messages. He called her every week to talk. He never once made her feel guilty for not coming to visit. He never once asked her to give up her adult life to be with him. But she'd felt bad anyway.

She got out of the car and retrieved her luggage from the trunk. As she approached, wheeling her suitcase behind her, a big smile surfaced on his ruddy face, making him look ten years younger than his sixty-five years.

"Hi, Daddy," she said. *Wow.* Whatever possessed her to call him that? She hadn't referred to him that way since she was a kid.

"Hey there, my girl. Welcome home."

As far as she was concerned, Thundering Hills, a large parcel of land to the west that was now incorporated into Rising Springs, had been her true home. Before the Boones got their hands on it. "Thank you."

She climbed the steps to come face-to-face with her father. He was pale and moving slowly but the light in his eyes was bright with excitement.

He opened his arms and took a step toward her, a shadow of fear crossing his face for a moment. He didn't trust that she'd embrace him. There'd been so many times in her young life when she'd needed a hug from him or a kind word, and he hadn't been there. For right now, she put that behind her. Well, as much as she could hope to. That kind of rejection was hard to forget.

She stepped into his arms and gave him a brief hug before backing away.

"It's good to see you, Drea. You look so pretty, just like your mama. You've been well?"

"Yes, I've been well. How about you, Dad?"

"Ah, I'm doing just fine."

She didn't believe him. He'd taken a fall and had downplayed it to her when she'd questioned him over the phone. He'd blamed it on a bad case of arthritis, but according to Katie he'd refused to go to the doctor for a health screening.

Back in the day, her father would lose his balance and crumble in a drunken stupor a few times a day. Now he probably feared she wouldn't believe he was clean and sober if he admitted to falling down the steps.

God, she hoped he wasn't backsliding. Not after all this time.

"We have a lot to catch up on, girl."

"Yes, we do. Let's go inside. I'll make us some dinner."

Her father's eyes brightened. "It's already done. I made your favorite, pot roast and red potatoes. I even attempted your mama's special biscuits."

"You did?" Nobody made homemade biscuits like her mother. Maybe Katie was right. Maybe her father was really trying. She could count on her fingers and toes how many meals her father had actually cooked for her as a child.

"Well, let's go inside and try them out," she said. "I'm starving."

"Sounds good to me. My stomach's been growling. But mostly I'm just pleased to have my little girl back home."

She was twenty-nine years old, hardly a little girl anymore, but she was here now and she'd have to deal with old memories and the pain those reminders evoked.

She forged into the house, wheeling her suitcase easily as her father followed behind her.

The next evening, Drea breathed a sigh of relief as she arrived back at the cottage after a very productive Mason-free day at the hospital. All day long she'd held her breath, thinking she'd run into him and have to make nice for appearance's sake, but he was a no-show and she was glad of the things she'd accomplished without having to deal with him. She'd gone over some important aspects of the fund-raiser with the supervisors of various departments and had called to confirm donors for the art sale. The rest of the event details involved the Boones and she had no other option than to deal with Mason on that.

She walked into her bedroom, left untouched since she'd lived here, and shed her business suit and high heels for a comfy pair of washed out jeans and an I ♥ New York T-shirt she'd received for running a 5K race. After pulling her hair up in a ponytail, she washed her face and brushed her teeth. Man oh man, she thought, glancing in the mirror. There was no denying she looked like a schoolgirl again. It was amazing how a little makeup and a sleek hairstyle could transform her appearance. But inside, she was still that unsure, guarded little girl.

At least it wasn't horrible living here, and her father was making a gold-star effort on her behalf. She was trying like hell to keep an open mind, trying to put the past behind her, but her scars ran deep and it wasn't easy to forgive and forget all she'd gone through here in Boone Springs. Not a day went by that she didn't think about the baby she'd lost, about the child she would never know. It wasn't Mason's baby, yet she'd blamed him for rejecting her, destroying her confidence and causing her to run into the arms of the first man who'd showed interest in her.

A knock at her bedroom door shook her out of her thoughts. "Drea, can I speak to you?"

She opened the door and glanced at her father. Beyond him, down the hall, she saw four men standing in the parlor. What were Mason and Risk Boone doing here? The ranch foreman, Joe Buckley, and Dwayne, one of the crew, were also there. "Sure. What's going on?"

Her father shook his head, his expression contrite. "I forgot about the poker game. We, uh, the boys usually come here on Tuesday nights. I'm sorry, Drea. I guess I've been so wrapped up in you being home, it slipped my mind. Should I send them away?"

"No, Dad. Of course not. I don't want my being here disrupting your routine." The irony was that as a kid, she'd always felt like a disruption in his life. She got in the way of his drinking.

"They brought dinner. Pizza from Villa Antonio. Will you come out and eat with us?"

What could she say? She liked Joe; he'd always been decent to her, and Dwayne was her age. They'd gone to school together. She didn't like breaking bread with the Boones, but she was hungry and she couldn't hide out in her room all night. "I suppose I can do that."

She walked into the parlor with her father and the men took off their hats. Everyone said hello but Mason. Hat in hand, he gave her a long stare and nodded.

"You still breaking hearts in New York, Drea?" Risk asked, his wide smile almost infectious. Risk was a charmer and she'd always been a little wary of him. He was too smooth for her liking.

"I don't know about that, but I like to think I'm killing it in other ways."

"I bet you are."

"Good to see you, Drea. You're looking well," Joe said. "It's been a while."

"Yeah, it has," she said. "How's Mary Lou?"

"Doing fine."

"Please tell her hello for me."

"Will do," he said, smiling.

"Hey, Drea," Dwayne said. "Missed you at the ten-year reunion."

"I know. I just couldn't get away, but Katie caught me up to speed on everyone. Congrats, I heard you just had a baby."

"We did. Heather and I named him Benjamin, after my father." He took out his phone and showed her a picture of his son.

"He's precious."

"We think so, too. Thanks."

"So you and Mason are gonna work together on the fund-raiser." Risk shifted his glance from her to his brother, a twinkle in his eye. Was he trying to cause trouble, or just being Risk? She didn't know how much his family knew about her history with Mason. True, it was old news. But not for her.

"That's the plan," Mason said, eyeballing her. "After the game tonight, I'd like to talk to you about it."

"We don't usually finish up too late," her father interjected. "It's a workday for everyone tomorrow."

"Okay, fine." She'd just have to put on her big girl panties. She couldn't postpone it any longer. She'd gotten herself into this and she had a job to do.

Mason gave her a nod and they all sat down at the dining room table. As she chewed her pizza and drank iced tea, every so often she'd steal a glance Mason's way, and each time, his coal-black eyes were on her, as if she was the only person in the room. He made her jumpy. She didn't like it one bit, and she fought the feeling.

But there'd always been *something* between her and Mason. Well, maybe it was all one-sided. At age seventeen her feelings had started out as hero worship for a guy six years older than her and had grown from there. Until he'd shot her down and humiliated her.

After dinner, the men got serious about poker, and Drea busied herself cleaning the kitchen, collecting and trashing pizza boxes and setting the coffeemaker timer to brew a dark rich roast in two hours. The guys had brought beer, something Drea knew her father had insisted upon. He wasn't going to spoil their night because he had a drinking problem. A tall glass of iced tea sat in front of her dad and he seemed fine with it.

Three years clean and sober.

God, she hoped the worst was behind him now. But there was always doubt in her mind, and maybe her father was trying to make a point by showing her he was a changed man.

During the game, she disappeared into her room and flipped open her laptop. She stared at the screensaver, a golden Hawaiian sunrise, wishing she could jump right into the picture.

But no, that wasn't going to ever happen. Was that kind of serenity even real?

She clicked open her spreadsheet and calendar and got busy working on items for the fund-raiser. There were dozens of moving parts for the big push and she was beginning to make headway.

After twenty minutes or so, she was totally engrossed in her work. A knock at her door broke her concentration and she jumped.

It wasn't her father's light rapping. No, she knew who it was. *Ugh*. She got up and yanked open the door, ready to face Mason.

Immediately the woodsy scent of his cologne wafted to her as she looked into his dark eyes. It was hard to miss the broad expanse of his chest as he braced his arms against her doorjamb, making her feel slightly trapped. "Hi," he said.

She'd expected him to be demanding, to insist they get to work, to pressure her. But that one word, spoken softly, surprised her and her defenses went up. "Mason."

"I, uh, I know it's late, but we should probably talk. If that's okay with you?"

It wasn't late. It was barely nine thirty. On really busy days, she'd often work until midnight. But things in Boone Springs were different than the big city. The pace was slower, the nights shorter, and the mornings came earlier. "It's fine."

"It's a nice night. Why don't you grab a jacket and meet me out back?"

She blinked. She didn't want to be alone with Mason on a moonlit night, but she wasn't about to show fear.

"Your dad's probably tired. I wouldn't want to keep him up with our chatter," he explained.

"Right," she said. "Give me a minute and I'll meet you outside."

Mason nodded and took his leave.

Drea shut the door and leaned against it, her pulse pounding in her ears.

Memories flashed through her mind, but she halted them in their tracks. She had a job to do. She was vying for a vice president position at Solutions Inc. A lot was riding on her communication and marketing skills with this fund-raiser.

And she couldn't allow Mason Boone to get in her way.

The screen door opened and Drea stepped outside. Mason shot up from his seat the second he glimpsed her. Her boots clicked on the deck as she approached. She was wearing jeans and a pretty pink blouse underneath a black leather jacket. Her hair was pulled back in a ponytail, with a few wavy strands falling loose, caressing her cheeks. She looked soft and pretty, so different than the uptight, buttoned-to-the-neck woman he'd met in the committee room yesterday.

Years ago, he'd been attracted to her for a short

time, until rational sense had kicked in and he'd backed off from the hell storm it would create. At seventeen, Andrea MacDonald had looked at him with adoring eyes and his ego had taken flight. But she was Drew's daughter, a mixed-up girl yearning for affection. Affection that couldn't come from Mason. He'd been twenty-three, six years older than her, and supposedly wiser. He would've only screwed her up more.

Now, he wanted to tell her she had nothing to fear from him, that he was dead inside and had been for a couple years, ever since Larissa died. But that was assuming too much. Maybe her coolness wasn't necessarily aimed at him. Maybe she'd changed from that sweet, caring, innocent girl she'd been to someone he didn't know, didn't recognize. Lord knew, he'd changed over the years as well, and he was simply here to work alongside her. The past was the past and maybe it was better to let it alone.

"Brought you some coffee," he said, grabbing for the cup on the wicker table beside him.

She smiled, apparently surprised at the gesture. "Thanks."

"I didn't know how you like it."

"Black is fine."

He handed it to her, their fingers brushing in the transfer, and he gazed into her pretty eyes. She lowered her lids and looked away. Those sage-green eyes were the same as Drew's, and her long, lustrous dark hair and olive skin were all her mother, Maria. Drea was a striking mix of Irish and Latina.

"You want to have a seat?" He gestured toward

the bench he'd been sitting on. He could feel her reluctance, sensing she'd rather have a root canal than sit with him, but she finally perched on one end. He sat as far away from her as possible, which was all of twenty-four inches, if that.

"So, you still resent all the Boones?" he asked on impulse. The question had been bugging him since he'd laid eyes on her yesterday.

Her head snapped up and coffee sloshed in her cup. Luckily, it didn't spill onto her hand. He would've never forgiven himself for that.

"Some more than others." Her eyes narrowed on him and suddenly she wasn't looking quite so pretty anymore.

"We tried to help your father, Drea. He was in desperate need and—"

"I know the story your family tells. I don't need to hear it from you."

"Maybe you do. Maybe that's the only way this is going to work between me and you."

"So, I'm supposed to forget all about the fact that when my father came to yours, asking for help with Thundering Hills, asking for a loan to tide us over for a few months, he was flat-out refused. Our families had been friends for years. And then, the next thing I know our land was bought out from under us and all we got were crumbs. Dad had to swallow his pride and take a job on Rising Springs. I had to move off our land to come live in this little cottage. We lost everything."

"That's not the way it happened, Drea."

"That's the way I see it, Mason. Total betrayal."

"Your dad…"

"What? What about my dad? He took to drinking heavily after mom died and…he's never been the same."

Mason didn't have the heart to tell Drea the truth. If Drew hadn't after all these years, then it wasn't his place to tell her that her little girl's perception of what happened had been all wrong. Drew had made Mason's father promise not to reveal details of the deal. Since both of Mason's folks were gone now, victims of a small plane crash years ago, he felt it was up to him to see that vow was upheld. If Drew wasn't willing to set his daughter straight, Mason surely wasn't going to do it.

"Drew's doing real good now." It was all he would say on the matter.

"So everyone in Boone Springs is telling me."

Mason didn't understand her. He was just barely coming out of his own grief, and related to how Drew MacDonald had been in the same situation, losing his wife the way he had, so unexpectedly. Mason hadn't taken to drinking the way Drew had, but everyone coped with heartache differently. He wasn't excusing Drew's bad behavior, but he knew what the man had been feeling.

Mason shook his head. "Aren't you glad he's getting better?"

"Of course I am. If it's the real thing this time." Her voice lowered to a whisper. "I've been disappointed before."

Mason ran his hand down his face. "I know it wasn't easy on you, Drea."

She shook her head, and he took in how her long hair flowed in natural waves down her back. "You know nothing about me, Mason."

He met her sad green eyes and something shifted in his heart. She tried to talk tough, but she wore her pain on her sleeve and her vulnerability grabbed him. "I know more than you think."

"That's a Boone for you, claiming to know every—"

He pressed two fingers to her lips, quieting her tirade. "Shh, Drea."

Her eyes snapped to his.

He couldn't believe he'd done it, touched her this way. But grazing her soft lips, looking into those defiant eyes was like a live wire sparking and jolting inside the dead parts of him. He felt alive for the first time in years. It was heady and he wanted more. He wanted to hold on to that spark that told him he was a living, breathing man.

Sliding his fingers off her mouth, he cradled her face, his thumb circling her cheek, strands of her hair caressing the back of his hand.

"Mason, are you crazy?" she whispered, yet the look in her eyes told him she was thinking something different.

"Maybe."

"You're not going to—"

"Yes, I think I am."

He put his mouth to hers and tasted her sweetness, the plump ripe lips that were meant to be kissed. Sensation flooded him. He remembered her. As a teen. A girl who'd needed affection, and he'd given it to her without question, until the night that she'd bared her soul to him and offered her body.

He'd had to turn her away.

Any decent man would have.

But she wasn't a kid anymore. And it was good, so damn good that instant guilt flooded him. His heart belonged to another and always would. That jolt of life he felt worried him and scared him silly. It was as if he was losing his wife all over again. He hadn't done anything this impulsive in years, much less with Drea, the very last woman on earth he should be kissing.

Two

Drea's mouth trembled as Mason brushed his lips over hers. She couldn't believe this was happening. She didn't want this. She didn't want him, even though his lips were firm and delicious, scented by coffee and the fresh night air.

He grabbed her upper arms, demanding more of the kiss. Her heartbeats raced, her body warmed and a sudden realization dawned. Whatever she and Mason had between them hadn't completely disappeared. It was real and hot and almost too out of control, but no, she couldn't do this. In the past, he'd caused her to do crazy, impulsive things. Her infatuation with him had almost ruined her life and she couldn't forget that. Ever. She squeezed her eyes tight, laid her hand flat on his chest and pushed as hard as she could.

He reared back, startled. "Damn, Drea."

"Mason, I don't know what you think you were doing—"

"The same thing you were. Kissing."

"I didn't w*ant* to kiss you." She'd wanted to slap his face, but…she wasn't a drama queen. The push sent the same message.

"I didn't want to kiss you, either. Okay, I did, but only in the moment."

"I thought you were a grieving widower." Her hand flew to her mouth, but the damage was done. She couldn't take it back.

He stared at her, his eyes losing their brightness. "I am," he said quietly.

Then why kiss her? "I'm…confused, trying to make sense of this. It was…unexpected."

"I know. For me, too."

She folded her arms over her chest, her lips slightly bruised from his kiss. "You had no right."

"I know that, too."

"Why did you?" She searched his eyes, saw raw emotion there.

"I, uh… You want honesty?"

"Always."

He ran his hand down his face again, stroked his chin. "I felt something. Something that wasn't dead inside me. Something that came to life the second I touched you, and I wanted to continue feeling it, even for a few more seconds."

"Oh, wow." She understood. Sort of. He'd been happily married with a baby on the way. And suddenly, it had all been taken away. She'd known that kind of loss, too, impetuously running into the arms of the first man she'd met after Mason rejected her, and getting pregnant. She'd lost that child in a miscarriage and walked away from Brad Williamson, the man who'd loved her. That year had been the hardest in her life.

And now what shocked her the most about all this was that *she'd* been the one to make Mason feel something. How was that possible? "Why…me?"

He smiled crookedly and shook his head. "I have no idea."

"Well, that's honest."

"Why did you kiss me back?"

She wasn't going there. She wouldn't tell him how much he'd once meant to her. How painful it had been when she was seventeen. And how much she resented him now because he'd made her feel something, too. "You're a good kisser."

"That's it?"

"Of course that's it. I haven't dated in a while and…"

"Okay, I get it." He blew out a breath and jammed his fingers into his hair. He seemed frustrated and a little bit angry. "Listen, let's forget this ever happened."

"Amen to that. So what now?"

"Now we do what we came out here to do. Talk about the fund-raiser."

"Okay, I guess we have no choice."

Mason frowned and she felt a little triumphant. At

least he wouldn't try to kiss her again. That would be a big mistake on his part, and an even a bigger mistake for her. As long as he kept his hands off her, she'd be fine. She took a big breath, willing her racing heart to calm down.

"So, where do we begin?" he asked.

"With me telling you my ideas and you thinking they're all incredible."

Half an hour later, Mason said good-night to Drea in the kitchen and waited until she headed off to her room, before grabbing another cup of coffee.

"You having more?" Drew said, coming in from the parlor.

"Yeah, if that's okay. We didn't disturb you. Did we?"

"Nah, not tired enough to sleep. Thought I'd get some coffee and sit for a while. I think I'll join you."

Mason knew how the older man liked his coffee. He poured him a cup, stirred in two lumps of sugar and handed it to him. Drew had a sweet tooth but it was harmless enough, a substitute for alcohol perhaps. "Actually, I was hoping to talk to you for a bit," Mason said. "If you're up to it."

"Winning always perks me right up. I figure I'm good for a few more minutes while I drink this mud. You and Drea were out there awhile. Everything good between you two?" he asked.

Mason had kissed Drea. He wasn't sure if he'd ever forget the spark that had lit him up inside like fireworks on the Fourth of July. So no, everything was not good. Drea didn't like him much, and he, well, he was feeling a hefty dose of guilt now, like he'd cheated on his wife. That gnawing ache wasn't going away and he doubted he'd get much sleep tonight. "Yeah, everything's fine. She's a smart woman. She's focused on the fund-raiser."

"She tell you all her ideas then?"

"She did. They're right on target. She seems to know how put on an event and build momentum."

They'd kick off the weekend on Friday evening with the HeART Auction of Boone Springs, garnering donations from local and not so local artists to sell on-site. For Saturday, she was planning a Family FUNd-raiser Festival, full of games and pony rides and raffles for children. Saturday night was reserved for a dinner-dance and she was in negotiations with a Grammy-nominated young country band to provide the entertainment. She'd managed to enlist a talented designer to create a website and was in the process of soliciting volunteers for the event.

Mason would be in charge of logistics and overseeing the big picture, while Drea and her committees would work on the details.

Their thirty-minute talk after they'd locked lips had managed to get his mind off her pretty green eyes and sweet body, and back on track.

"I'm sure proud of her, but I wish she'd let up a little bit."

"She only has a short time to make it all happen, Drew."

"I know, but is it selfish of me to want her to myself? I mean, I know I don't deserve it, and Lord knows, I'll spend the rest of my days trying to make up for being a lousy father to her when she needed me the most."

"She'll come around. She loves you, Drew."

"Yeah, but she doesn't always like me so very much."

Mason rubbed his jaw. Drea didn't like him, either, and maybe that was a good thing. It would keep him from making the mistake of kissing her again. But he wasn't one to give advice to Drew or anyone on matters of the heart, so he kept his mouth shut. "Aunt Lottie's back home. She arrived last night from her trip to Africa and she's thrilled that Drea's here. I think you can expect her to come for a visit."

"Lottie, huh? What the hell was she doing in Africa for all those months?"

Mason grinned. He suspected Drew was sweet on his aunt, but the two were like oil and water. And they had history: Lottie and Drew's late wife, Maria, had been best friends until the day she'd died. "Don't know. Maybe you should ask her when she stops by."

Drew looked away and grumbled something about her not wanting to see him.

"What?"

"Nothin'."

"Aunt Lottie wants to surprise Drea, so don't say anything to her, okay?"

"I won't say a thing. My lips are sealed."

"Dad, are you talking to yourself?" Drea wandered

into the kitchen and stopped short when she spotted Mason. "You're still here?"

He nodded, speechless. Drea was in her pajamas, a pair of soft pink cotton pants and a matching top that clung to her breasts, hiding little. His mouth was suddenly dry, but Mason kept his composure, even while that *alive feeling* bombarded him. "I was just going."

She folded her arms around her middle. If she thought that shielded her, she was mistaken. The material only pulled tighter across her chest.

Mason turned and brought his coffee mug to the sink. He couldn't look at her another second without showing her—and her *father*—how much she affected him.

He could hardly believe it. Drea had poked the sleeping bear and he needed to get out of here, pronto. He headed for the front door, keeping his back to the MacDonalds. "Thanks for the game tonight, Drew. Good night, Drea." Then he exited the cottage without giving either of them a parting glance.

The next day, Drea must've put a good one hundred miles on the car making stops all over the county, checking items off the to-do list on her cell phone. She'd be lost without her list. It was sort of scary thinking how if anything happened to her phone or tablet, her entire life would be erased. Lately, for this project, she'd been taking pen to paper, jotting notes as a backup, too. But her mind was crowded just the same with all the details for the event.

As she parked the car in the driveway of her father's cottage, she closed her eyes, thoughts running rampant through her head.

Check in with the caterers.

Make the rounds at local art galleries.

Double-check with Katie regarding the children's cupcake-decorating booth.

Plead with The Band Blue to donate an evening of entertainment.

Stop thinking about Mason.

Darn it. The more she tried, the harder it was. She'd be right in the middle of planning her next move with the fund-raiser when her mind would flash to Mason. His fingers softly touching her, the immediate red-hot spark that baffled them both and then the determination in his eyes when he'd finally bent his head and made exquisite contact with her lips. He'd stirred something deep inside her, more than curiosity, more than bravado, and she'd had to see the kiss through.

He'd said she made him feel alive. Now if that wasn't an ego boost. And she hadn't lied; it had been the best kiss she'd had in a long time. That was where it got confusing. She resented Mason. For how he'd humiliated her. For how he'd dismissed her so easily and broken her heart. She'd lost so much of herself then and had run into the arms of the first man who'd paid her attention, giving him her body, but not her heart.

A knock on the car window snapped her out of her thoughts. She opened her eyes and focused on the woman smiling in at her.

"Drea, sweetheart. I couldn't wait another second to see you. I hope I didn't startle you."

"Lottie?"

"It's me. I'm back and I'm dying to talk to you."

Drea couldn't get out fast enough to give her "aunt" a long, lingering hug. "Oh, Lottie. It's so good to see you!" Because Drea's mom and Lottie had been BFF all their lives, she'd been in Drea's life, too. After her mother died, Lottie had given her the love and attention Maria couldn't any longer.

Drea pulled back to look into Lottie's eyes. They still held sparkle and spunk. At sixty, Lottie was no wilting flower. She'd kept up her appearance, wearing trendy clothes, staying slender and coloring her gray a honey-blond shade, her silky locks reaching her shoulders. "You look beautiful, Lottie. I swear you never age."

"Age is just a number, sweetie. And that's so kind of you to say." Lottie smiled again, giving her the once-over. "You're the one who's beautiful, Drea. You're all grown up. I know I say that every time I see you, but it's true. You look more and more like your mama every day."

"I'll take that as a compliment."

"As well you should. Gosh, what has it been? Two years since I've seen you?"

"Yeah, two years. You came to visit me in New York."

"We had a great time, going to shows, shopping."

"It means a lot to me that we stay in touch." They'd

made an effort to call or text every month or so whenever Lottie wasn't traipsing around the globe.

"I promised I would."

"Hey, what's all the fuss about?" Drew came ambling out of the house.

Lottie rolled her eyes and whispered, "Your father has turned into an old man."

"I heard that, Lottie," Drew said with a scowl.

"I don't care if you did, Drew. It's true. You're not ready for the grave yet. Lose a few of those extra pounds you're carrying and see if you don't feel like a new man."

"Well, now you're my doctor, too. Did you learn all that in Africa?"

Lottie grinned. "Actually, I learned a lot of things on my trip. I spent a good deal of time on the tour bus with a homeopathic doctor, as it happens."

"Oh, yeah? Did he cure your ailments?"

"If I had any," Lottie said softly, "I'm sure Jonathan would've cured them."

Drew's eye twitched and just for a second his face grew pale. "Well, come in. You girls can jabber all you want inside the house."

Drew held the front door open for Lottie and Drea and they marched into the parlor. Lottie had brought them all a home-cooked dinner, Cajun chicken and shrimp pasta, her signature dish and one of Drea's favorites. It was warming on the stove.

Drew took a seat and listened to his daughter and Lottie chat about Broadway plays, clothes and music.

Whenever Lottie was around, Drew felt old. Her vibrancy and zest for life looked darn good on her. She was a pain in his rear end, but she was also a life-long friend. One who never ceased to speak her mind. Whenever she was gone, he missed her. And whenever she was home, he wished she'd keep her opinions of him to herself. He was tired, his bones ached, but listening to his daughter and Lottie chat lightened his mood.

"Dad, did Lottie tell you she went on safari?"

"She did."

"Sounds exciting, doesn't it?"

"Well… I suppose."

"It was a grand adventure," Lottie said, her soft brown eyes gleaming. "I loved every minute of it."

"But now you're home for a while, right?" Drea asked.

"Lord above, yes. I'm home for a good long time. Texas is in my blood. I missed it and my nephews."

The relief Drew felt gave him pause. Why was he so darn happy to have her home? Hell, whenever Lottie was around, his head became jumbled up with all sorts of mixed emotions.

"And I'm especially glad I'm back in time to see you." She took Drea's hand. She'd been more a mother to Drea than he'd been a father.

"How long are you here, honey?"

"I'll be staying for several weeks, putting together the fund-raiser for the hospital."

"Mason told me about it. You two are working together, so I know it'll be successful."

"I think dinner's just about ready," Drew announced.

"Gosh, I smell something delicious cooking," Drea said.

"It's Lottie's Cajun supper."

"Your favorite, Dad." Drea gave him a big smile, her eyes twinkling.

"As I recall, it's your favorite, too. And Lord knows, she wouldn't be fixin' anything so delicious if it was just me."

Lottie whipped her head his way. "Drew MacDonald, why are you always so disagreeable?"

"You saying you fixed that special meal on my account?"

Lottie rolled her eyes. She did that a lot and he found it annoyingly cute. "I'm saying we all like the dish, so why not dig in."

"Sounds great to me. I missed lunch and I'm starving." Drea stood and gave them both a quick glance.

"I've got the table set," Drew said. Well, Lottie had helped. She'd arrived just a few minutes before Drea got home and they'd worked quickly together. His heart flipped over the second he'd laid eyes on Lottie, after her being gone for so long, and he'd been a bit flustered ever since.

"Sounds good to me. I only hope the meal's as good as you two remember it."

"If you made it, Lottie, we're gonna love it." Drea eyed him, sending him a message to give Lottie his assurances, as well. But she didn't need any more encouragement, he decided. She was the strongest woman he knew.

As Lottie walked past him, arm in arm with his daughter, the woman's sweet, fruity scent teased his nostrils, reminding him of freshly picked strawberries. Oh man, it was going to be a long night.

The autumn sun arced over the horizon, shedding light and warmth on the morning. Drea squatted in the dirt and gave a good hard pull on one of the many weeds, gripping the base near the root with her gloved hands. The darn thing wouldn't budge. She'd be damned if it would get the better of her. She stared at it, as if hoping it would wilt under her intense scrutiny.

No such luck.

While she was here in Boone Springs she'd vowed to tidy up her father's neglected yard. Since her meetings didn't begin until eleven, today was a good day to get started.

"Okay, you monster, you're not getting the better of me." On her knees now, she tightened her grip and pulled with all her might. "You're going…down."

The weed popped from the earth and the momentum sent her flying back. She landed on her butt in a pile of wilted petunias. "Ow."

"Looks like the weed wasn't the only one going down."

She stared up, straight into Mason's face, and saw a smirk twitching the corners of his mouth. "Are you kidding me? Where did you come from?"

He put out his hand to help her up.

She ignored it, bracing her hands on the ground

and shooting to her feet, then dusting the dirt off her jeans. Why was this man always catching her in embarrassing situations?

"I usually run this way in the morning."

She took in his black jogging pants and snug white T-shirt. His arms were two blocks of muscle straining against the cotton material. It was sigh-worthy how good he looked this early in the morning. The whole package smacked of good health and vitality and…sexy man.

The truth was the truth. Mason was still handsome, but that one kiss the other night meant nothing to her. She clung to her resentment, because the alternative—getting hurt again—wasn't an option.

"I'll remember that," she said. She would make sure not to bump into him again at this hour.

"You're up early."

"Gardening, as you can see. My dad's been neglecting the grounds and I'm hoping to make a dent in all this."

"If I know you, you'll fix up this garden and make it shine." His words came with an approving gleam in his dark eyes.

"You sound so sure of yourself."

"I am."

"And you know that about me how?"

"I can see how hard you're working on the fundraiser. You won't stop until you reach your goal."

He was right. She was a woman on a mission. She'd never had much approval in her life, having to fight for everything she'd attained, without much recognition. Not that she'd needed constant glory, but a compliment now and then was always welcome. "Thank you."

He pushed his hand through his hair and gave her a solemn look. "Listen, we've sort of hit a snag with The Band Blue. I spoke with their agent last night and it doesn't look like it's going to happen for us."

"What? How can that be? They seemed interested last time we spoke."

"Yeah, about that. You spoke with Sean Manfred, the lead singer, and apparently the kid has a soft spot for our cause. His mother is a heart attack survivor and he wants to help, but their agent isn't onboard. He says the band couldn't possibly come until his demands are met."

"What are his demands?"

"He wouldn't say. He wants a sit-down to go over everything."

"That's fine. I can do that. I think when he hears how much good—"

"The thing is they've got a gig at the Hollywood Bowl in LA this weekend and their manager will only agree to a face-to-face meeting. I suppose he's trying to appease Sean, while making it harder on us. Frankly, we can't afford to waste any more time on this. If we can't get them to agree, we're dead in the water as far as entertainment goes on such short notice."

"We?"

"Yeah, we."

"I can handle it on my own, Mason."

"Showing up as a team will help persuade him. We can take my company plane, and besides, it'd give me a chance to check out a piece of property I've had my eye on."

"In Los Angeles?"

"Yeah, on the beach."

"I didn't know you were a beach kind of guy," she said matter-of-factly, while her heart pumped overtime. She'd have to spend a lot of time with Mason on the trip. It was business, but still…

"I'm not really, but maybe it's time for me to branch out a little. I mean, Larissa always loved the beach. Claimed it soothed her, gave her peace."

"And you can use a little of that?"

He shrugged. "Yeah, I guess."

He gazed down at Drea as if puzzling something out. Perhaps he was looking for inner peace, while his body craved vitality. She could understand that.

"So it's settled? We'll leave Saturday morning."

"Uh, sure. We'll be home Saturday night, right?"

Mason eyed her and she saw him calculating what they needed to accomplish in one day. It was a three-hour trip to Los Angeles. That meant six hours of flying in one day. "If the agent isn't being an asshole, we should be able to make it back in time." His eyes twinkled. "Do you have a hot date on Saturday?"

"Me? I have no time for dating. I'm concentrating all my efforts on the fund-raiser."

"Okay, then. I'll make the arrangements and let you get back to fighting weeds."

"Sounds…good." It didn't. She nibbled on her

lip, battling emotions. On the one hand, she really needed to nail down the entertainment for the night. She'd hit a brick wall on getting a band to agree, until she'd spoken with Sean. He'd made it seem as if there wouldn't be a problem; all they had to do was iron out a few details. But she should've gotten the okay from their agent first. Her mistake. Now she had to do some fast talking to secure their commitment. But on the other hand, traveling with Mason meant they'd be spending a full day together. She vowed not to let her ill feelings about him get in her way. "And I wish you'd stop doing that."

His brows pulled together. "Doing what?"

"Catching me in embarrassing situations." First the pajama thing and today her ungraceful battle with a weed.

His smirk spread into a wide smile. "Just lucky I guess." He took off jogging down the road and she stood there watching him slice through the wind with those long strides. An unwanted thrill ran through her body and she chewed on her lip, silently cursing the warmth filling her up inside.

Three

Saturday morning, Drea rose and double-checked her luggage making sure she packed her usual change of clothes just in case of an accidental spill or a delay, along with the necessary paperwork for the deal with The Band Blue.

Almost as important, she brought along her notes on her top five reasons it would be advantageous for the band to join in their fund-raising event. No one would ever call her lazy or doubt her determination. She'd done extensive research on the group and was prepared to use all the tools in her arsenal to get them to sign on the dotted line.

She showered and dressed in black slacks and a white bell-sleeve blouse, all the while going over her business strategy in her head. She'd wear her blazer during the meeting, but for now, a comfy cardigan would do for the plane ride. A pair of short beige boots completed the outfit.

She tiptoed into the kitchen and found her father up and dressed already. "Dad, you're up early." It was barely seven o'clock.

"That I am."

He tied the laces on a pair of walking shoes that looked brand-new.

"What's going on?"

"Lottie wants me to walk with her. Claims I need to get in shape."

"Oh, uh…"

He glanced at her and frowned. "I'm not so old I can't still get around, you know."

"But…you haven't been exercising. Maybe you should take it slow."

"If I don't go, Lottie's gonna keep pestering me."

"Dad, I think you're darn glad Lottie's here to pester you."

"I don't know. Maybe." He shrugged. "I'm meeting her at the main house in half an hour."

"Is it like a date?"

Her dad groaned as if she was insane. "It's a walk, period."

"Dad, I'm going out of town. What if…" She bit her tongue. She knew what he was going to say and couldn't very well stop him.

Her father finished tying his shoes and looked up at her. "I've been on my own a long time, Drea. Don't worry about me. I've gotten along all this time without you."

Bingo. It was true, so she couldn't argue with him on that.

"Okay, well, I'll probably be home late tonight. I'm going to California with Mason. We have hospital business."

"You need a suitcase for that?" Drew eyed her momentarily and she mentally cringed. She didn't want to think about spending the night with Mason, yet it was a possibility. But that didn't mean she had to pack her prettiest lingerie, a light sage nightie that barely covered her thighs. Why had she done that?

"I have papers in there, mostly. And a change of clothes, just in case, Dad."

Her father's pale green eyes lit up. "I bet Mason's hoping for *just in case.*"

"What? Don't be silly, Dad. He's the last man on earth…"

"He's hurting and you two go way back, Drea."

"It's business, Dad. You know I don't like the Boones, Mason most of all."

"All right, honey. If you say so."

She felt like she was ten years old again. "I say so. I'll text you before we take off."

"To make sure I survived the walk around the ranch?"

She smiled. "Making sure you survived Lottie's well-intentioned nagging."

That made her father grin. "That woman is a pain in my rear end."

"She's a sweetheart and you know it. You just give her grief."

"Turn that around, and it'd be true." But there was a lightness in his voice she hadn't heard in a long time.

There was a knock at the front door. "Sounds like Mason's here," her father said.

"I'll get it." Drea headed there through the parlor.

She found Mason dressed in a pair of crisp jeans and a snap-down shirt under a black jacket. Business casual. At least they were in tune in the apparel department. "Mornin'," he said in his sexy Texas drawl.

"Mason, I'll be right with you. Unless," she began, her manners getting the best of her, "you'd like to come in?"

"Come in, boy," her father called from the kitchen. "I've got a fresh pot of coffee going."

Mason eyed her outfit and hairdo. Maybe she should've put it up, instead of leaving her hair free to drape down her back. "Man, right about now, I'd kill for a cup." He glanced at his watch. "I think there's time. Our flight leaves at eight."

"Thank goodness," she said. "I'd kill for a cup, too." She let him in.

"A quick one. We'll have breakfast on the plane, so no worries there."

Drea bit back a snide comment. His company plane was just another classic reminder of losing Thundering Hills to the Boones. Mason spoke of it casually, as if normal everyday people could fly around in their own airplanes. The Boone empire had flourished, while her legacy, the land she'd loved, had been swept away.

Hastily, she poured them each a cup and listened while Mason and her father spoke about the weather, cattle prices and Lottie. "I'm afraid she's on a crusade," Mason said, grinning. "She spent some time with that doctor and now she thinks she can cure the world."

"Well, I'm gonna give it a go."

"Exercise never hurts. But be warned, next she might tackle your diet."

"That'd be the day."

"Mason," Drea said, slurping the last sip of her coffee. "We should probably go."

"Yeah, I've gotta get a move on, too," her dad said. "You be sure to take good care of my girl while you're gone. Okay, son?"

"Dad!" She sucked in a quick breath. "I don't need Mason or anyone else taking care of me. I'm perfectly cap—"

"Yes, sir," Mason interrupted. "I'll be sure to keep her safe."

Drea shook her head and kissed her father on the cheek. "Don't strain yourself today."

"I'll be just fine. You have a good trip now."

Mason grabbed her luggage in the parlor and then held the door for her. "All set?"

As much as she was going to be. "Yes."

He put his hand to her lower back and guided her to a shiny black limousine in the driveway. The warm contact felt too good. She stiffened up and focused her gaze on the uniformed driver standing at attention beside the car.

"I've got this," Mason said to him. He put her luggage in the back and then gestured to the open door. "After you."

She slid inside and he followed. His presence seemed to fill the lush leather interior, and she was surprised at how little physical space there was on the seat between them.

She'd seen the inside of a limousine exactly four times. The first had been during her mother's funeral. That had tainted her perception of limos for life. The ride had been the hardest she'd ever taken. She hadn't been able to look at her father's ashen face another second, so during the drive she'd stared out the window in utter silence, her young heart breaking.

Who ever said limos were fun?

"Let's head to the airport," Mason told the driver.

She glanced over at him, noting how he seemed to be in total control of his environment. She could really respect the business side of Mason. He was focused and driven. She'd dwell on that aspect during her time with him and not think about his pleasing musky scent. Or how the sunlight seemed to catch the inky strands of his hair in just the right way. Or how intense his dark brown eyes were. No, she'd concentrate on her newly thought up theme, *Business with Mason.*

"Just so you know, I can keep myself safe. I don't need you protecting me."

He grinned. "I know that. I was humoring your father."

"Oh." She sank back in her seat. Should she believe him? It didn't matter. She knew the truth. She'd been taking care of herself for a very long time now.

She spared him another glance. His eyes were twinkling, as if he found her amusing.

She tried to drum up anger or resentment, but neither emotion surfaced. She hated to admit it, but he'd been sweet to consider her father's feelings.

And who would've thought she'd ever associate the word *sweet* with Mason's name?

"Comfortable?" Mason asked, sitting down across from her on the plane.

The white leather seats were wide and luxurious. A small table separated them. She was aware of the stocked liquor bar behind her and a television screen on the opposite wall. The flight attendant had just taken her order for breakfast.

"Yes."

"Okay, we'll be taking off soon."

"At your command," she said.

He stared at her and put a finger to his eye, struggling not to frown. "Drea, what?"

"Nothing."

She smiled. She was a master at hiding her demons, but somehow being with Mason made them all come out again. "I'm fine."

"Fear of flying?"

Fear of Boone. "No, nothing like that. I think I'm just hungry."

"Breakfast is coming right up."

The pilot's voice came over the speaker. He explained the flight route and weather conditions and asked them to put on their seat belts. Shortly after, the plane began to taxi on the runway.

She and Mason were quiet until they were airborne.

"Here you go. I hope you enjoy this. It's one of Mr. Boone's favorites." The flight attendant presented her with a vegetable egg white scramble and a cup of coffee. Mason had the same.

"Looks wonderful, thank you," Drea said.

The stewardess walked off and Mason began digging in.

"So, you really think we can get The Band Blue to sign on the dotted line?" he asked her.

"With my people skills, yeah, I do."

"You have people skills? You mean the way you charmed me?"

He was teasing, but he'd caught her red-handed. "I'm not a phony."

"You mean if you liked me a little more, I'd know it? Never mind," he said, dropping the subject. "So how did you come upon fund-raising as a career?"

"It was accidental, actually. My college roommate came down with a rare type of lung disease in our senior year. It was pretty serious and she needed treatments that required hundreds of thousands of dollars, treatments that her insurance didn't cover. I knew I had to help her. I gathered up a bunch of her friends and fellow students and started a fund-raising page on social media. I wrote articles for the local newspapers and even did a morning show with Sandra's parents to bring awareness and raise funds. Within a matter of weeks, we had more than enough money for her procedures."

"Impressive. How is your friend now?"

"She's doing well. There's no cure for her condition, but she has a good quality of life and I was just invited to her wedding."

"Nice. You saved her life."

"Not me, the doctors."

"You're being modest."

"I wish there was something I could've done for my mother, though. I know I was just a kid, but I always think that maybe my father and I missed something. Her heart attack came on so suddenly and we never had a clue she had heart disease. She had no symptoms and, well, after that first attack there was so much damage..."

Drea lowered her head as emotions whipped through her system. Her mother had lasted only three days after the attack. And Drea wished she'd said more to her, wished she'd realized that she was losing her, wished she'd told her how much she loved her. Instead, everyone had tried to protect her, to make it seem that Maria MacDonald was going to be fine, when they'd probably all known differently.

Drea didn't know why she'd exposed herself to Mason this way. She never talked about her mother's illness, much less confided in a man she thought of as the enemy. She lifted her eyes and found pain in Mason's expression.

"Yeah, I know what you mean," he replied.

"Mason, I'm sorry." His pain had to be more raw. More fresh. He'd lost his wife and unborn child to heart failure just two years ago.

Drea reached out to him, put her hand over his. It was instinctive, a move she'd afford anyone in pain. The connection flowed between them, strong, powerful, sorrowful. She resented the hell out of him, hated what his family had done to hers, but in a moment of shared grief, she'd forgotten all that. And then she pulled her hand away. *Business with Mason.*

"All through here?" The stewardess appeared, ready to remove the plates.

"Yes, all through," she said.

"Would either of you like more coffee?"

"No," they answered simultaneously.

"Okay, if I can get you anything else, Mr. Boone, please let me know."

He nodded. "Thank you."

The flight attendant went back to her station and Drea was left alone with Mason once again. "You know, I think I'll stretch my legs."

Why not? The plane was roomy enough to move around in and she needed space.

When she stood, Mason stood, too, his Southern manners on full display. As she started to walk past him, the plane lurched and she was tossed against his chest. Immediately, he wrapped his arms around her. Even after the quick bout of turbulence was over, Mason didn't let go.

"You okay?" he whispered in her ear.

"Uh-huh."

From where she was nestled in his arms, the slightest hint of his masculine cologne teased her nose. She closed her eyes, enjoying a few seconds of comfort. "Thanks for the catch."

"My baseball days come in handy."

"Tee-ball?"

"College. All Star."

"Of course. You wouldn't be anything else."

Her snarky remark brought a chuckle. "You make me laugh, Drea."

He skimmed his hands over her back, stroking her ever so gently, bringing her closer. His legs pressed against hers. She didn't want to know what a brush against his groin would bring. She didn't want this. But her heart was pounding and the strength of him, his *maleness*, sent thrills careening through her body.

The plane lurched again, this time breaking them apart. Mason reached for her, but she was too far from his grasp. It seemed the stratosphere had more sense than either of them.

"Sorry about that, folks," the pilot said over the loudspeaker. "There shouldn't be any further turbulence. You can relax and enjoy the rest of the flight."

"Good news," Mason said, but his words belied the dangerous gleam in his eyes.

Drea grabbed her bag from where she'd been sitting and pointed to a sofa a few feet away. "I think I'll just sit over there for a while. I…have some work to go over."

While Mason watched, she moved as gracefully as

she could down the aisle and then plopped onto the sofa and avoided him for the rest of the trip.

A few hours later, as she and Mason were driving down the highway in a rented Cadillac SUV, breathing California air and enjoying West Coast sunshine, his cell phone rang. He tossed her the device. "Can you get that for me, please?"

Drea picked it up and glanced at the screen. "It's the agent," she said to Mason before answering. "Hello, this is Drea MacDonald."

"Hello, Drea. Alan Nesbitt here."

"Yes, Mr. Nesbitt. We've just landed and we're on our way."

"That's why I'm calling. I'm afraid I can't do lunch today. Something's come up that I have to deal with. I hate to do this to you, but it can't be helped."

"But we've flown in from Texas. And we need to speak with you."

"Yes, yes. That's fine. I don't have a spare minute until after the show."

"You mean tonight?"

"Yes, the band goes on right before the headliner. We can talk then. I'm afraid that's all that I can do. I'm swamped today."

"Okay, we'll come to the show."

"I'll leave VIP tickets and backstage passes for you. We'll have a good hour to talk then."

"I guess that will have to do. We'll be there. This is important."

"I understand. I'll see you tonight."

Drea pushed the off button and faced Mason. "He's canceled lunch."

"I heard."

"He claims he has time to see us tonight at the show."

Mason frowned. "We have to give it a try. What else can we do? We're here already."

"I agree. But now we have a lot of time to kill. What are we going to do for eight hours?" Drea was not happy about this. She and Mason would be spending the entire day together. And after what almost happened between them on the plane, she had to be on guard.

"I can think of a few things," he said cryptically. Yet there was no villainous arch of his brows or twitch of his lips. When she didn't respond, he asked, "Are you hungry?"

"I'm not starving, but I could eat."

He nodded. "Me, too. Do you like seafood?"

"Who doesn't?" She actually loved it. When she was in college, she'd go for Friday night fish frys with her friends. It was always something she'd looked forward to.

"Great." At the next signal, Mason whipped the car around. "I know this little place on the beach I think you'd like."

And soon they were on Pacific Coast Highway, the ocean to her left and the cliffs to her right. The homes on both sides of the road had amazing views of the sea. "Have you have been to LA before?" Mason asked.

"Yes, once, but I never saw the outside of my hotel."

His brows arched and he glanced at her.

"I was attending a conference," she explained. Not that it was any of his business how she'd spent her time here. "So yes, technically I've been here, but not enough to get a West Coast vibe."

"I think I can remedy that."

It didn't sound awful so she nodded. "Okay."

A few minutes later, Mason pulled into the parking lot of an outdoor café. Big Fish was a small take-out restaurant with picnic tables and café chairs facing the water. "Not fancy," he said, "but the fish are fresh and everything is delicious."

After being on the plane for three hours and then in the car this past hour, sitting outside in the autumn sunshine sounded pretty good. "I'm game."

They got out of the car, Drea stepping down before Mason could open the door for her. She wasn't a feminist really, and understood he was just displaying his ingrained Southern manners, but she was perfectly capable of getting out of a vehicle without his assistance. Still, he put his hand to her back and guided her through the parking lot to the take-out window. She glanced at the chalkboard menu on the wall. "What do you recommend?"

"If you love shrimp and scallops, their Big Fish Special is pretty good. Everything comes with fries and coleslaw."

There wasn't a salad on the menu. Or a fruit plate. She decided to throw caution to the wind today and go for broke. "I'll have the Big Fish Special then, thank you."

"Make that two," Mason said to the lady behind the window.

When the food was ready, they walked over to a picnic table near the water. Drea took a seat and Mason slid in next to her. Both wore their sunglasses and silly bibs around their necks while they enjoyed the food. She had to admit Mason didn't look intimidating now; his body was relaxed, his hair swept back by the slight breeze, his usual glower gone.

"This was a good idea," she said, plucking up the last of her French fries.

"You mean I did something right for a change?"

She caught the twinkle in his eye. "All I mean is you have good taste in food, period."

"I figured."

"So, what's the plan now?"

Mason glanced at his watch. "It's a little after one." They still had several hours before the meeting. "How do you feel about carnivals?"

"Carnivals?"

"Santa Monica-style. We'll hit the pier next. It's not far from here. If you've never been, it's worth seeing. And I promise you, they have the best ice cream on the beach."

"It's your nickel," she said. "I'm going along for the ride."

A short time later, Drea had settled on a cup of strawberry ice cream and was spooning small bites into her mouth as they relaxed on the Santa Monica pier.

Mason shook his head at her choice of dessert. "You're no fun."

"I'm a lot of fun," she said, "when I want to be."

He held a mouthwatering double-fudge-brownie ice cream waffle cone in his hand. They stood against the guardrail overlooking the ocean, listening to the lapping waves hitting the shore. It was something they didn't get in their part of Texas.

"Oh yeah? When do you want to be?"

His eyes were on her, watching her lick the cream from her spoon. It unsettled her, the gleam in his eyes, the sudden flirty tone in his voice. "When I..."

"When you what?"

He seemed intent on her answer. "Well, not now. Today is all about business." At least it should be.

"We're taking a business break...out of necessity." She blinked.

"This is a no-business zone," he continued. "Look at the people here. Think they're worried about numbers, spreadsheets, their boss's latest tirade? No, ma'am. I don't think so."

He did have a point. "So if this is a no-business zone, do you mind sharing some of your double-fudge-brownie ice cream?"

"It depends," he said. "What do I get in return?"

"What do you...uh, what do you want?" A memory flashed of being nearly naked in his bedroom, craving his kisses, wanting his touch. She didn't allow those recollections often, but today they came easily, and for a second she was reminded of the good parts of that memory. How it felt when he'd released her hair from her braid. He'd weaved his fingers through it, as if the strands mesmerized him. And how it felt to be in his arms, his lips on hers, his body hot and demanding. She'd never known a greater desire in her young life than anticipating making love with him. But it had ended there. Mason had put a stop to it, and she was left with only rejection and humiliation.

"A ride."

She blinked, pulling herself back to the present. "What kind of ride?" Back then, there was only one she'd wanted from Mason.

"Take your pick." He nodded toward the amusement park attractions behind them. The hum of laughter, mechanical noises and screams merged in her head. It was the sound of good, honest fun.

"But I get my ice cream first?"

"Fine."

She went in with her spoon and he backed away. "You can't eat a cone with a spoon. Take a big bite and enjoy it."

He offered her the side he hadn't licked yet. But still, wasn't it too intimate to be sharing ice cream this way?

The I-dare-you look in Mason's eyes sparked a desire to prove something to him. She grabbed the cone out of his hand and dug in, taking a bite of the waffle and the dreamy chocolate ice cream in one big mouthful. She'd literally bitten off more than she could chew and Mason's eyes were on her, watching her deal with it, watching her mouth move inelegantly. Then he laughed and his well-hidden dimples appeared. There was a brightness in his expression she hadn't seen since they were much younger. He lifted a napkin to her lips, catching a drop of ice cream.

Their eyes connected then, and there was a moment of intense awareness.

He was touching her face again, standing close enough for her to see the coal-black rim around his deep dark eyes. Close enough to see his jaw tighten suddenly, to see his expression change. She felt it, too. Every time he touched her, she felt desire. Here, with dozens of people milling about on the pier, it was as if they were the only two people on the beach. If he bent his head and leaned in, would she allow him to kiss her again?

"Excuse me, miss. Would you mind taking our picture?" A woman stepped up, unaware that her interruption had just prevented them from making another mistake. Drea should have been relieved. Instead she didn't know how she felt. Let down, maybe. The woman waited patiently, holding a cell phone in her hand. Adorable twin boys stood beside her.

"Of course. I'd be happy to," Drea answered, handing Mason back his cone.

With the beach at her back, the woman ushered her two boys in front of her and Drea snapped the picture.

"Thank you," she told Drea, then took off with the children.

Mason stepped up. "Let's take that ride now."

Getting chummy with Mason put her nerves on edge. She didn't want to enjoy the day so much, and in the back of her mind she was second-guessing all her decisions. While she wanted to stick to her *Business with Mason resolution*, he was trying his hardest to change it into a no-business zone.

"Well?" he asked, watching her closely. "Have you decided?"

She turned around to peer at the rides and made a decision. "I'd like to try the Pacific Wheel. I overheard someone saying it's the only solar-powered Ferris wheel in the world."

He shook his head. "Boring."

"Boring? But you said it was my choice?"

"That's before you slurped up half my ice cream cone. I figure you owe me."

Of course Mason wouldn't play fair. She knew that about him. "I do, do I? Why don't I like the sound of that?"

He led the way. "C'mon. Let's see what the Pacific Plunge is all about."

Mason drove down Pacific Coast Highway with Drea beside him in the passenger seat. Her hand was braced on her midsection, which she rubbed every so often. She hadn't wanted to go on that ride; he'd seen it on her face, the fear, the doubt. Yet she'd been a trouper, bravely getting on the contraption that lifted them up ninety feet over the water. He'd wanted her to see the view from the highest point of the pier, and it had been amazing. But then, as promised, once they'd reached the top, they'd plunged. Other people had screamed and laughed as they went down. But not Drea. She'd turned the same shade of green as her pretty eyes. Once they'd touched ground he'd helped her off the ride as she'd clutched her queasy stomach.

"Feeling any better?" he asked, taking his eyes off the road to look her way.

"A little." She adjusted herself in her seat. "I'll be fine. The fresh air is helping. Even if it didn't end well, I'm okay with taking the plunge."

"I'm glad. It was fun."

"For you, maybe."

He sighed. Drea wasn't giving an inch, but he knew darn well she had enjoyed getting a little taste of the beach town. "I meant, I'd hoped it was fun for you, too. I'm glad you're feeling better."

"Thanks," she said simply.

Hell, Mason couldn't remember the last time he'd felt so carefree, but he focused on the drive now, since Drea seemed to be lost in thought.

Ten minutes later, she asked, "So, are you meeting a Realtor at the beach house?"

He shook his head. "No. I have the keys."

"Is that a privilege of the rich and famous? You get keys to homes you're thinking of buying?"

"I'm not famous."

"Gee, I don't know too many people who have whole towns named after them."

"My family settled Boone Springs decades ago," he told her. "*They* built the town, not me. I'm not going to apologize for them." He couldn't hide the pride in his voice or miss the pout forming on Drea's mouth.

Right now that pouty mouth looked very kissable. Ever since he'd kissed her that night, he'd had mental flashes of how wonderful it had been to touch his lips to hers, to taste her sweetness.

Yet, every night, his heart ached for his wife. He missed her like crazy and so these unexpected thoughts of Drea were confusing the hell out of him. Part of him wanted to hold on to the guilt and sadness, but another part was trying to break free. It was all so new to him and he could only go with what felt right in the moment.

She remained silent. He knew what she thought about his family. She had no warm feelings for any of them, with the exception of Aunt Lottie. Drea had misconceptions and so much hurt buried deep inside, he didn't know if she'd ever find resolution or peace. So he let the subject drop. Today wasn't the day to be on a Boone family soapbox.

"Actually, the beach house belongs to a business associate of mine. She was nice enough to overnight me the keys so I could look the place over at my leisure."

"Have you been here before?"

He almost heard the "with her" in her question.

"Yeah, I have been. Once. Missy coaxed me to come out and stay here shortly after Larissa passed."

"Missy? I see. So you stayed with her?"

"I did."

He glanced at Drea and she immediately looked away, concealing her expression from him. But her face had turned that green shade again. Was it disapproval? Disappointment? Jealousy?

Thinking of her being jealous made him smile

inside. Maybe she'd been fantasizing about him a little bit, too.

"For a few days, yeah. Missy needed me almost as much as I needed her."

Slowly, Drea nodded, as she fiddled with straightening her blouse. She wouldn't look him in the eye.

"Missy's husband had passed, just about the same time my wife… Uh, anyway, after her grandchildren showed up to the beach house, I went home."

"Grandchildren?"

Mason grinned. "Yeah, she has five of them, as I recall. Did I mention Missy's in her seventies?"

"No," Drea said, then cleared her throat. "You left that part out."

"Well, she's an incredible woman."

Drea's eyes narrowed on him. Had he deliberately led her down a merry path? Maybe. He sort of liked thinking she'd been jealous.

"You know, you're a—"

He gave his head a shake. "Uh-uh, Drea. Don't say it."

Her shoulders slumped. "You're right. I won't."

Mason kept a straight face, but inside he was actually grinning.

Four

The beach house, two stories of gorgeous space, smart styling and incredible views, was set on a shelf of land just above the ocean. Drea looked out on the waves as the fall sun began to lower to the horizon. Ten steps led down to the sandy shore, where the water foamed only thirty feet away.

"It's perfect," Drea mumbled.

Mason placed a glass of white wine in her hand as he came up behind her. "Now it's perfect," he said.

Both of them watched the waves hit the shore, and quietly sipped wine.

After several minutes, Mason asked, "I take it you like this place?"

She turned to look into his eyes. He seemed genuinely interested in her opinion. "What's not to like?"

He shrugged. "It's different than Texas."

"Isn't that the point? You'd use it as a getaway, right?"

He shrugged again. "I'm…not sure."

"Then why are we here? I mean, why are you considering buying this house, if you don't think you'll be comfortable here?"

Mason finished his wine and set his glass down on the white wooden railing. Both floors had a wraparound veranda.

"It's hard to explain. I feel as if I need to do something to move forward with my life. I thought a change of pace, something new, might help me figure it out."

He stared at her, as if wondering why he'd told her something so intimate. Most of the men she'd known weren't forthright in sharing their innermost thoughts. Was he sorry he'd confessed this to her?

"It's weird, right?" he asked, doubt evident in his eyes.

"No. Not weird at all." She didn't want to sympathize with Mason. It was crucial to hold on to her anger and indignation and never let it go. Because her life hadn't been peachy, either. Not only had she lost her home, her mother, and her father to alcohol, she'd lost something even more precious.

A baby.

"Hey, are you okay?" Mason tipped her chin up so he could meet her eyes.

Sincere concern washed over his features, frightening her. She didn't want to be friends with Mason.

She didn't want his concern. Quickly, she snapped out of her musings. "Sure, I'm fine."

She faked a smile and turned to walk into the house, but he grabbed her hand, halting her retreat. "Would you look at that." He pointed to the ocean. Following his gaze, she glanced at the water and saw a frolicking school of dolphins close to the shore, their smooth, silvery forms rising up from the water and then diving back down, making perfectly shaped arches. Up and down, up and down.

"Wow, I've never seen this in person."

Mason tugged on her hand. "Let's go get a better look. You game?"

"I'm game."

Once they were both barefoot, Mason led the way down to the beach, where sand squished between her toes. The air was cooler by the ocean and beaming sunlight cast a beautiful sheen on the water. Breezes kicked up as she kept her eyes trained on the dolphins swimming by. She stood stock-still, watching them until they faded from sight. "That was something."

"It's pretty incredible." Mason glanced along the empty beach. "I'd like to take a walk before we have to leave. Care to join me?"

She wanted to say no, to put some time and space between them, but when would she ever get another chance to stroll a Pacific beach? "I think I'll tag along."

They walked along the shore, with the foamy waves inching up the sand and teasing their feet. She'd never been a beachgoer, but this little game of keep-away was fun.

Until she stepped on something sharp. It jabbed at her right foot, catching her off guard. "Ow!"

She stumbled, and Mason rescued her midway before she fell, grabbing her waist and righting her. "You okay?"

"I think so. I stepped on a seashell or something buried in the sand."

Mason looked around. "You're right. It was a seashell."

He held her still, his hands clamped around her waist. Ocean breezes swept his hair back and ruffled his shirt. As they stood facing each other for a moment, a monumental thrill scurried down her spine. He was incredibly handsome like this, appealing in a way she didn't really want to admit.

She was about to tell him that maybe the cowboy was also a beachcomber, but her lips parted and nothing came out. When Mason's gaze slid to her mouth, a little gasp escaped her throat. Before she could utter a word, he pulled her closer, bent his head and delivered a gift to her lips. It was so pure, so natural a gesture, with them standing on the deserted beach, the sun lowering on the horizon and all the planets aligning, that she didn't think to stop the kiss. Or him.

He pressed his mouth more firmly now, and she parted her lips in a gasp of pure pleasure. He wasted no time inserting his tongue and tasting her, shocking her senses in the very best way. His kiss shot hot beams of pleasure straight through her, and if that wasn't enough, his arm snaked around to bring her even closer. Her legs were touching his, with her hips against his groin and her breasts pressed to his chest, She was willing and at his mercy.

Yes, Mason knew how to kiss.

He knew where to touch her to elicit a needy response, too.

He wove his free hand through her hair.

His other hand dropped from her waist, his long fingers inching down to graze her rear end. *Oh God.* She craved his touch, wanted more, wanted to stay like this a good long time.

His masterful kiss did that to her.

They were molded together, lip-locked and fully engaged. She felt his shaft, thick and hard, pressing against her. It didn't surprise her to feel it, but what did surprise her was her total acceptance of the situation.

She sighed deeply, majorly turned on but confused all the same.

"Don't think," Mason whispered, as if reading her thoughts. "I'm not."

He nipped at her lower lip and then drove his tongue into her mouth again.

I'm not thinking. I'm not thinking.

When the kiss finally ended, Mason's dark eyes probed hers. He reached out to touch the side of her face, his fingers a gentle caress on her cheek. "Thank you," he said softly.

She blinked. Instead of saying *that was amazing*, or *you're beautiful* or *wow*, Mason was thanking her?

And then it hit her like a ton of bricks. She made

him feel "alive." He'd already admitted she'd been the only woman to make him feel that way. *So far.*

She could turn him on. Make him hard. Get his juices flowing.

Yet she couldn't help feeling used. Slightly. It pissed her off a bit.

She didn't want to be Mason's *test kitchen.*

She didn't want to be Mason's anything.

His phone alarm buzzed and he reached into his pocket and pushed a button on his cell to shut it off. "It's time to go. There could be traffic."

She nodded, speechless, and when he grabbed for her hand, she pretended not to see it and jogged up to the house. Once she was on the veranda, she turned to him as he approached the steps.

"Just so you know, thanking me wasn't necessary. You're a good kisser, Mason. And like I've said before, it's been a long time since I've been kissed."

His eyes narrowed. She whirled around before she had to acknowledge the deep frown surfacing on his face.

It was definitely safer to harbor resentment for Mason.

But it sure wasn't as easy as it had once been.

Electricity charged the air at the Hollywood Bowl that night. The iconic outdoor stadium in the Hollywood Hills held a huge crowd of country music fans. A person might think she was back in Texas for all the cowboy hats, silver belt buckles and snakeskin boots filling the arena. Drea's sour mood lifted the second she entered the place and they were shown to their center stage seats. She had to hand it to Mr. Nesbitt.

They'd arrived just in time to see The Band Blue walk onstage amid a roar of cheers. To be the opening act at the Hollywood Bowl was huge. Landing a commitment from the band would almost surely guarantee the fund-raiser's success. She understood that Nesbitt was just doing his job; she understood his hesitation. From this point on, their careers depended on visibility. Drea just had to make sure Nesbitt would see it her way. At least she had Sean Manfred, the lead vocalist, in her corner. The kid had an amazing voice.

During the performance, she found Mason's eyes on her. Too often. It was as if he was puzzling her out. But her puzzle pieces didn't fit with his and it was time she made that clear to him.

No more hand holding. No more kisses. No more intimate conversations.

Business with Mason.

She sat with her hands in her lap, swaying to the music and applauding when the songs ended. The Band Blue drew a noisy crowd bordering on rowdy. But it was all in good fun and she found herself really enjoying the music.

Thirty minutes in, Sean angled his guitar to his side and spoke into the mic. "Thank y'all for coming. The band and I, well, we sure do appreciate your support."

"We love you," a woman shouted from behind Drea.

Sean chuckled. "We love you guys, too. And now, if you're ready, we're gonna end our night with a song

I think you'll recognize. Recently, my mama took sick with her heart, but she's one of the lucky ones. She survived."

Drea drew a deep breath. Mason glanced at her, his eyes soft, and for a second—okay maybe more than a second—she connected with him emotionally.

Sean went on. "So tonight I'm dedicating this here song to my mama. Love you, Bethy Manfred," he said. The crowd shouted words of support and adoration, and then quieted as the band began to play.

When the sweet love ballad called "Your Heart Is Mine" was over, Sean thanked the crowd again before the lights dimmed and the band walked off.

"Time to get backstage," Mason said.

Drea rose and Mason ushered her down the aisle and over to the backstage door. They showed their VIP passes and were immediately let into a special room. A buffet table lined one wall and they were told to help themselves. Drea grabbed a bottle of water and took occasional sips.

Finally, the band entered the room, led by a guy who couldn't have been more than thirty years old. He actually looked like he belonged in the band, with his wispy blond hair and casual dress. He took a look at Drea and Mason, then immediately walked over, while the band members hit the refreshment table. "I'm Alan Nesbitt," he said, no smile, all business.

"I'm Drea Macdonald."

"Mason Boone." The two men shook hands.

"The show was spectacular," she said.

Alan shook his head. "It's always a challenge with

outdoor acoustics, but yeah, the boys did real good. Would you like to sit down?" He gestured to a group of tables. "We have a bit of time before they go on for an encore performance with Rusty Bonner."

The conversation was stilted and one-sided, and Alan didn't seem to want to make any allowances. He called the band a hot property and said that right now they needed to keep their options open.

"I understand all that," Drea said. "But what if we promised you they'd get a ton of exposure? And don't forget the goodwill this charity would invoke."

"Listen, I'm not hard-hearted, but there are costs involved. We'd need a place to stay, since traveling with a band is expensive. These boys have played for pennies, and now's their big chance. We're just gaining momentum."

"Okay, so you'd need a place to stay and travel expenses." She glanced at Mason and he nodded. "Got that covered. What else?"

"We need maximum exposure. This is a small-ass town, right? Who's gonna see them perform?"

"We can accommodate about five hundred people on the grounds."

"Did you see the size of the Bowl? Try five thousand for starters."

"Yeah, but Boone County is full of larger-than-life Texas donors. These are people who have connections all over the globe. Isn't it all about networking?"

Alan's brows lifted. "Keep talking."

"This fund-raiser is a big deal for the community. There'd be a lot of local news coverage."

"Understood."

"So what if we auctioned off one of the band members for a date with a fan? We could start promoting it now, and by the time the event rolled around, you'd have a ton of exposure, and the fund-raiser would get an added boost, as well."

"I'm volunteering to do it," Sean said, walking over to the table. "I think it's a great idea. And… I'm single at the moment." A crooked grin spread across his face. He was probably twenty at best.

He put out his hand to Mason first. "Hi, I'm Sean." They shook and then he turned to her. "You must be Drea MacDonald. Nice meeting you in person, ma'am."

Drea smiled. "Same here."

"Yeah, uh, I'm sorry about what happened to your mom, Miss MacDonald. Losing her like you did must've been very hard."

"It was. Still is," she said honestly.

"I like the date idea," Alan said quietly, considering it. "It's a good marketing ploy."

"If you agree, I promise no one will work harder to get the coverage you want than I will," Drea declared. "I'll write up a press release tomorrow."

"I'd like to help your cause." Sean looked at his agent. "I've been telling Alan that we should do this. It's important. Chances are my mother wouldn't be here today if she hadn't had excellent cardiac care. I spent a lot of time in the hospital chapel praying for her recovery. I think this is a way I can give back and make good on the promises I made that day."

If Drea had liked this young man before, now she adored him. "Thank you, Sean. And it *is* important." She glanced at Mason. "Many of us have lost loved ones."

Mason's expression softened, his gaze touching hers. She hated the effect he had on her. Tonight she wanted no distractions.

"My family owns a hotel in Boone Springs," Mason said to Alan. "We'd be happy to put you all up. And I can make sure the company plane is available to fly the band in."

Alan Nesbitt's expression changed, his skepticism replaced with consideration. She'd done all she could to address his main concerns, and luckily, the group had that weekend free. This might work out, after all.

The rest of the band members walked over and stood around the table. "It's a good gig," the drummer said. "I'm in."

The others nodded.

"We've got the details covered," Drea said. "Now we just need an agreement. And I happen to have something written up here in my briefcase."

Drea felt as if she was floating on air, spreading her arms like wings and gliding through the parking lot. She'd signed the deal with the band. "Can you believe it?"

Mason grinned. "You were amazing in there. You had a comeback for every single one of Nesbitt's demands. I'm impressed."

"Now we can go back to Texas with clear heads."

"Yeah, we can." Mason glanced at his watch. "But not tonight."

"What?" Drea stopped in her tracks.

"I told my pilot if we didn't need him by 10:00 p.m. to go to bed and rest up. It's only fair. We'll have to take off in the morning."

"What time is it?"

"Eleven thirty."

"Oh, wow. I didn't realize how late it was." Sean had asked them to stay for the final song of the night, when the band joined the headliner, Rusty Bonner, and Drea had been happy to agree. "Can we get a hotel at this hour?"

"We could try. But the beach house is twenty minutes from here. We could be there faster than trying to find rooms on a Saturday night."

Drea eyed him carefully.

"There's five bedrooms, Drea. You can sleep downstairs and I'll—"

"I get it." She wasn't worried. The house was enormous, and all she wanted to do was plop her head on a pillow and get some sleep. It had been a long day. "It would be cool to wake up in the morning at the beach."

Mason nodded and they took off immediately. The drive to the house was traffic free. When they got there, he parked the car and grabbed their bags. They entered the house quietly; the gentle roar of the ocean was the only sound in Drea's ears. She welcomed the peace and quiet.

"Pick a room down here," he said. "I'll check things

out before turning in upstairs." Their eyes met. Mason hesitated briefly, as if he wanted to say something, but then thought better of it. "Good night, Drea."

"Night," she said. "See you in the morning."

Drea entered a bedroom decorated in dove blues and grays, the furniture sleek and modern with sharp lines. The contemporary feel of the place was so different from anything Mason Boone was accustomed to in Texas. She had a hard time picturing him being happy here. There was too much Texan in his bones.

She unpacked her bag, taking out fresh underwear and her nightie, and walked into the bathroom. What had she been thinking, bringing her finest lingerie on this business trip? She chuckled at the absurdity. After that kiss today on this very beach, Drea knew better. The kiss had only reinforced her resolve to steer clear of Mason. As soon as she was back on Texas soil, her focus would be on the fund-raiser, and not on Mason's swoon-worthy body and masterful kisses.

After undressing, she showered quickly. Then she dabbed herself dry with an ultrasoft towel, donned her sage nightie and crawled into bed.

Pure heaven.

Closing her eyes, she sank down into the comfy mattress and settled in.

Minutes later, a piercing alarm brought her head up from a sound sleep. She glanced at her surroundings, disoriented, until she finally remembered where she was. The alarm rang louder, more urgently.

"It's okay, Drea," she heard Mason call over the deafening noise.

She rose and opened her door just as she heard a crash in the other room. "Ow! Damn it."

"Mason?" She ran into the living room and found a shadowy form pushing up from the floor, then hopping on one foot. "What on earth?"

"Hang on a second," he shouted above the blaring alarm. He limped over to the hallway wall and punched a code into the security system. The harsh ringing immediately stopped. Turning, he explained. "Sorry. I, uh, couldn't sleep and decided to get some air. I forgot I'd set the alarm and when I ran inside to shut it off, I knocked over a lamp."

"Are you hurt?" she whispered.

"Just my pride," he said.

In the darkness she could barely make him out.

"Let me take a look." She found a light switch and clicked it on. When she turned back to Mason, the expression on his face faltered as he looked her up and down. His mouth dropped open and a fiery heat filled his eyes.

"Holy hell, Drea," he rasped.

Oh yeah, her slinky nightie.

He cleared his throat. "Is that what you wear to bed?"

His chest was bare, his pants dipping well below his waist. She swallowed, her heart racing, his hard body disturbing her sanity.

"No, I, uh…yes. Sometimes."

"Sometimes, meaning when you're on a business trip with me?"

"Don't flatter yourself."

"I'm not. I'm...*grateful*."

"I just grabbed the first thing I found." What a lie. "Let's just forget about this."

"Don't think I'll ever forget it."

She closed her eyes. She was drawn to him in inexplicable ways, and right now her body was calling the shots. Seeing that look in his eyes wrecked her good sense. She spun around. She couldn't submit to him. She hated him. She...she didn't want him or anything to do with the Boones.

"Don't go, Drea."

She squeezed her eyes tighter. Her feet wouldn't move. "This isn't going to work," she murmured. She couldn't possibly cave, not after all that had happened—or rather, hadn't happened—between them years ago, all that had changed the path of her life.

"We have the night. One night, Drea. Here. You and me."

"There is no you and me."

"There could be."

"Mason, we can't do this. There are things you don't know. Things that make this impossible." Why was he being so persistent? Why wouldn't he just let her go? Maybe for the same reason she'd packed her sexiest nightie for this trip. Maybe there was something that needed finishing.

"All I see are possibilities tonight."

He was pleading his case, countering every one of her refusals. It was hard saying no to him. Not when her body cried out for him. To know Mason that way one time. Would that be a punishable crime?

She pivoted around slowly and Mason was there, in front of her, his eyes raking her in as if he'd already touched her. As if he was making love to her with his deep dark gaze.

Just once. Just once. Maybe she needed to finish this.

Yet she wanted to scream at the injustice. She hated him more because she *wanted* him.

Mason knew the exact moment Drea decided their destiny tonight. It was in the sudden release of tension in her shoulders, the parting of her sweet lips, the tiny, almost imperceptible nod of her head.

He reached for her hand. "Come with me."

"Where?" she whispered.

"Upstairs."

Without another word, she took his hand and he led her up the staircase to the room he'd chosen to sleep in. The bed was massive, but that wasn't why this space spoke to him. He'd slept in big beds before, but never one with a wall-to-wall window looking out to the ocean and a big beautiful moon. It was as exquisite as a painting. And to have Drea here, set against this stunning backdrop, only heightened the moment, heightened his arousal, made him ache for her. "You're beautiful, Drea."

She looked away, out the window to the seascape. She was still unsure.

"Just one night," he promised. He couldn't take anything more. His heart wasn't healed yet and he didn't know if it would ever be. But Drea woke something in him and he couldn't let it go. He couldn't stop what was about to happen between them.

Taking her hand, he placed it flat on his chest, right over his heart. Her body trembled and her lips quivered.

Was she remembering the last time they'd been like this? Ready to make love, until his brain finally clicked in. It seemed like a lifetime ago. He'd wanted her then, but she'd been young and pure, a virgin, and Drew's daughter.

Tonight was different. She was no longer that young, insecure girl who'd needed affection, who'd needed to feel loved. Drea was all woman, decisive, someone who knew what she wanted. Even though she was reluctant, she would have walked out the door if she truly didn't want to be here with him.

Right now her sweet palm was on his skin and he burned for her touch. He had been empty for so long, but Drea was filling him up, making him overflow with need.

No other woman had done that to him. Not since Larissa.

Tomorrow he might regret this encounter. Tomorrow they'd have to forget all about this and go back to working on the fund-raiser. But not now. Tonight was about the two of them finally coming together.

Just once.

Her fingers glided over his chest. He sucked in oxygen and moved closer to her, giving her better access to his body. "Oh man, Drea."

She put her lips to his chest and her lustrous black

hair fell forward. He spread his fingers through the strands as Drea's mouth skimmed over him, licking, kissing, gently, timidly.

She was driving him insane.

He tipped her chin up and brought his mouth down, tasting her sweetness. Her lips were soft and plump, and deserved to be ravaged.

A tiny moan escaped her throat, proof that she wanted things to move faster. His body was on fire and each kiss brought them closer and closer to… more.

All he could think about was getting her naked and touching every single part of her. "I'm glad you wore this," he murmured, slipping a finger under one strap of her sexy gown.

"Why?" she asked, sounding innocent.

"Because I'm dying to take it off you."

"Mason?"

He lowered the strap all the way down her arm, then did the same to the other, allowing. her gorgeous, perfectly rounded breasts to pop free. It was suddenly hard for him to breathe. "Wow."

She smiled and wrapped her arms around his neck, causing all that beautiful softness to crash into his chest. His skin burned hot where her nipples pressed against him, and he struggled for control. He kissed her once more, then moved her back against the window and undressed her, removing the flimsy garment carefully.

"You've got it off me," she whispered. "Now what are you going to do with me?"

"Are you kidding me, sweetheart? What am I not gonna do with you?"

"Hmm. I like the sound of—"

He brushed his mouth over hers again, impatient and yearning to touch her. Then he whipped her around so that she faced the window, her back to him, and cupped her breasts in his palms, stroking her again and again. He kissed the nape of her neck and watched her reflection in the window as she opened her mouth to gasp, to smile, then squeezed her eyes shut at the pleasure. His thumb flicked one rosy peak, then the other, and she squirmed in his tight hold. "Drea, open your eyes and look out. It's—"

"Stunning." She gazed out at the glistening water, and then her eyes met his in the reflection from the window. "You're a devil," she whispered, fully aware now that he'd been watching her. "I've never…" She didn't finish her thought, but she wasn't backing off, wasn't angry. Instead, there was awe in her voice.

"Don't close your eyes, Drea. Try to keep them open."

She nodded, the back of her head gently knocking into him.

He rained kisses along her shoulder blade and then slid his palm down her torso, leaving the comfort of her beautiful breasts, seeking another comfort below her waist.

She jumped when he touched her there. "You okay?" he asked.

"Oh, I'm perfect," she murmured, meeting his gaze again in the window, her eyes smoky.

"I can't disagree, darlin'."

And then he began a slow deliberate stroking, eliciting whimpering moans from her. She was so ready, so willing, and he wanted to go on making love to her this way.

In just a matter of minutes, she came apart, and he witnessed the pleasure on her face, knowing full well he'd given that to her.

She turned around and fell into his arms. He clasped her to him and held on tight. It seemed so natural with her, like it was meant to be.

Then he lifted her up and carried her to the bed.

The night was just beginning.

Five

Drea lay on the bed, not quite believing what had just happened with Mason. It was so much more than she'd expected. Now she had to face her new reality: she'd just given in to the enemy and liked it. How monumental was that? And how did she feel about Mason now?

He stood by the bed, his eyes dark, bold and dangerous, totally wiping out her long-ago fantasies of him. He was better than anything her young mind could've conjured up. But back then, it had been about more than sex. Then, it had been about love.

Mason unzipped his pants and pulled them down, never once looking away from her.

A lump formed in her throat. Her body immediately revved up again when she saw him fully unclothed for the first time. All that bronzed skin and muscle. Below the waist, he was pretty awesome, too. He caught her eyeballing him and smiled, but she didn't care. She wasn't a kid anymore. She knew lust and desire, and if this was her only night with Mason Boone, she wasn't going to hold back. "Come to bed," she demanded.

"Bossy," he said with a wide, gorgeous grin. "Are you always like this in bed?"

She chewed on her lower lip and went for the truth. "I'm never this way…in bed."

"Then I think I like it."

He placed one knee on the bed and the mattress dipped. The reality of what was happening hit her, but she focused her attention on him, his masculine beauty, this drop-dead handsome guy covering her body with his.

Every touch, every caress was thought out, meant to bring them both the greatest amount of pleasure. He played the boss game with her, asking her what next, what did she want from him, and he obliged, but deep down she knew Mason wasn't a pushover. He was in full control at all times. And secretly, it turned her on even more.

She wanted to think of this as an impulsive, quick encounter, one they'd both probably come to regret later on, but there was nothing impulsive about the way Mason made love to her. He was slow and deliberate and knew exactly how to make her cry out, how to make her want more, how to make her forget everything but what was happening right now.

"Tell me when you're ready," he murmured against her throat.

"I'm ready," she blurted.

He pressed a kiss to her mouth. His face was a picture of sheer lust and promise.

"Hang on, darlin'," he said, leaning over the bed. He rummaged through his pants pocket and came up with protection.

"Do you always bring those with you?" she teased, watching him rip open the packet.

"I grabbed them at the last minute," he said. "Sorta like how you brought along that slinky piece of fluff you were wearing tonight."

She smiled. Wasn't he clever. "How many *did* you bring?"

"Three." And then he was settling over her body, laying claim, joining them together in a hot flurry of lust and craving.

Drea lay in the crook of Mason's arm, her head resting on his shoulder, her body drained, all her energy spent. She didn't know how long she'd been resting against him. She must've dozed off for a time. Clouds partially covered the moon now and through light and shadows she saw the steady rise and fall of his chest.

She considered going downstairs to sleep in her designated bed, because somehow, sleeping like this with him seemed far too intimate. Yes, they'd taken liberties with each other tonight, but that was about sex. And this was about intimacy and closeness.

She still didn't know Mason any better than she had before.

Except to say he was better than good in the sack.

Her decision made, she slowly backed off, slinking away from the warmth of his arms.

But he pulled her closer. "Drea, where are you going?"

"To…to my own bed."

He sat up then, and urged her to do the same. She kept a sheet around her nude body, covering her to the neck. His eyes dipped there and he frowned slightly. "Why?"

"Because…it's for the best."

"You know what's best? Getting something to eat. I'm starving," he said. "You must be hungry, too."

Now that she thought about it, they really hadn't had much of anything to eat since having lunch at Big Fish. "I am a little bit hungry."

"Missy keeps the fridge semistocked."

"We can't just eat her food."

"Sure we can. I'll replace everything. I owe her for the busted lamp, too."

Mason swung his legs over the bed and stood up. He wasn't shy, that was for sure. She had a great view of his backside as he slipped on his pants. He grabbed his shirt and stepped around her side of the bed to hand it to her. "Come on, Drea. The night's not over yet. Let's raid the fridge."

According to the digital clock on the nightstand, it was 2:15, the middle of the night, for heaven's sake. But Mason bent his head and kissed her softly on the lips, and her arguments dissolved. There was still some time left before this magical night would end. "Turn around."

His brows shot up. "You're kidding, right?"

He had a point. There wasn't any part of her body he hadn't caressed or kissed, so she shouldn't be shy with him. "I'm not kidding."

He didn't argue as he turned away from her, which gained him a brownie point. She rose and slipped on his shirt; it almost reached her knees. Her fingers quickly worked the buttons all the way up to her throat. "Okay."

He turned and nodded. "Cute." He took her hand in his and they went down the stairs together, bumping bodies in the dark and chuckling about it.

Once in the kitchen, they set the dimmer switch to soft lighting. Mason opened the fridge and she peeked around him to see inside.

"Eggs, bacon, bread, milk," he said.

"Do you like French toast?"

He looked back at her. "You willing to make it?"

"I am. I might cook up some bacon, too."

"I didn't think this night could get any better," he said. He sounded serious and his tone sent shivers through her body. He wasn't teasing. He wasn't making a joke. So far it had been a pretty spectacular day *and* night, yet everything about it scared her silly.

She reached past him and grabbed the bacon. "I'll get this started."

When she turned, he was there, smiling. "Drea, you're an amazing woman."

"Tell me that after you try my French toast."

He curled his hand around her neck and kissed her, hard. When he finally let her go, she rocked back on her heels, her heart hammering.

"You could burn the damn toast and you'd still be amazing."

She felt a blush coming on. Was she that good in bed, or was it that she was the first woman he'd been with since his wife? Could that be true?

Had he been celibate for two years?

She was getting too deep inside her head. That wasn't good. This was a one-time thing and in the morning she'd go back to being cranky Drea from New York and he'd be the man she loved to hate.

Things would get back to normal.

"Uh, thanks," she said, then set about searching for a pan to fry the bacon.

Ten minutes later, she flipped the French toast on the griddle while the bacon cooled on a plate. Mason came up behind her, lifted her long hair and planted tiny kisses behind her ear and along her neckline. Ever since they'd come downstairs, he'd found ways to touch and kiss her while she cooked. And each time, her heart raced and her mind flashed on how he'd made her feel upstairs in the bedroom.

"Did you set the table?" she asked softly.

"All done," he said.

She dished up a platter of brioche French toast halves and bacon, and turned toward the table. "You're only halfway done, Mason. You only set out one plate."

He took the platter out of her hand, set it down and

then sat in front of that one place setting. "One plate is all we're gonna need, darlin'."

"What are you—"

"Come here." He grabbed her hand and guided her down onto his lap.

Her body nestled into his easily and he placed a hand on her thighs. "Comfy?"

She laughed. "Are you serious? You want me to feed you?"

"My stomach's growling, but you get the first bite." He lifted a strip of bacon to her mouth.

She hesitated half a second, looking into his eager eyes, then took a small bite. After chewing and swallowing, she offered a piece to him. He gobbled a big mouthful chewing with gusto like a little boy getting his first taste of candy.

"Mmm."

"You like my bacon?" she asked.

His mouth twitched, a wicked gleam entering his eyes. "Very much."

She caught his meaning and shook her head.

They took turns feeding each other in the dimly lit kitchen, munching on French toast and bacon in between sweet kisses until most of the food was gone. Mason's body reacted every time she moved on his lap. His large hand held her in place as he stroked her thighs with the flat of his other palm. Her skin prickled and moisture pooled at the apex of her legs. Beneath her, Mason's body was hard, his shaft nudging her side. Her breaths came faster now, and he caught her mouth and kissed her thoroughly until they were both breathless.

"Drea, sweetheart," he whispered hastily, lifting her body and turning her so she straddled him on the chair.

His hands worked underneath her shirt and he tormented her unmercifully.

There was no hope for it. She gave him everything she had, and when he joined their bodies again, her release was instantaneous and damn near glorious.

And when they were through in the kitchen, Mason carried her upstairs to the bed. "The night's not over yet," he promised.

They still had two hours before the dawn of a new day.

Drea doodled on a pad, drawing irregular circles and juvenile-looking flowers, her mind a million miles away from her fund-raising update that would begin in ten minutes in the hospital boardroom. Her lists were all prepared, but it hadn't been easy concentrating on the task. She had Mason Boone on the brain and she kept reliving the magical night they'd shared in California. She would probably never top those twenty-four hours. She and Mason had allowed themselves a brief interlude and made the most of it.

One night.

That's what they'd agreed on.

She'd reminded Mason of that as they'd left the beach house two days ago. Two days of not seeing Mason by her request. She'd insisted on delegating duties and carrying them out separately. He hadn't argued, but her gut told her Mason didn't like it much.

It had made for a long, tense plane ride home. No touching, no teasing, no easy conversation.

And now her body ached, yearning for what was forbidden.

"Good morning, Miss MacDonald. Am I too early for the meeting?"

Her head snapped up at the sound of the female voice. She faced a pretty blonde woman dressed impeccably in a pencil skirt similar to the one she was wearing. "No, not at all. Please call me Drea. We're all working toward the same goal here."

"All right, Drea. Nice to meet you. I'm Linda Sullivan. I missed the initial meeting, but I've been briefed. I'll be your go-to publicity person."

"Great, we're gonna need you. Our financial goal is lofty, but I think we can do it. Are you on the hospital staff?"

"Oh no. I don't have a medical background. I work for Boone Inc. Mason Boone sent me over to help out."

"Oh, so he's not coming?" A dose of relief washed over her.

"That I don't know. He told me about your incredible idea to raffle off a date with the singer from The Band Blue. I've been working behind the scenes and have already contacted their agent. We're putting our heads together on some ideas."

"Okay, great. Sean is a great kid and so are the

other band members. We're lucky to have them. So I'm hoping we can make this happen seamlessly."

"I'll do my best," she said.

"Is Mason your boss?"

"I work for all three of the Boones, but mostly for Mason. Risk does some traveling for the company and Lucas was just recently discharged from the military. He's working his way back into the family business, I guess. Mason is pretty awesome to work for."

Drea tilted her head. "How so?"

Linda shrugged. "He's…nice. Not just to me, but to everyone in the office. You know, he seems to really care about his employees."

"Does he?" She sounded skeptical and Linda gave her a funny look.

"Sure he does. When my mama took ill, he gave me all the time off I needed and then called me once a week to make sure I was okay."

Drea didn't want to hear this. She didn't want Linda's hero-worship of her boss to sway her opinion of the Boones. Especially Mason. "I'm sorry to hear your mom was ill."

"She's recovered now and living a good life again."

"I'm glad."

The committee members and volunteers began filing into the conference room, greeting Drea as they took their seats. Once they were settled, she rose to address them.

"Hello, ladies and gentlemen. Thank you for coming. I'm pleased to say that because of all of your hard work, the fund-raising event is shaping up nicely.

We're right on target and things are really coming together. I'm thrilled that The Band Blue has agreed to be a part of the festivities, with an added bonus. We'll be raffling off a dream date with Sean Manfred, the lead singer of the band, to one lucky fan. We're hoping this will spark more interest and bring in more revenue for the hospital."

She spoke to the volunteers in charge of the game booths and the art auction, and introduced Linda Sullivan to everyone. Linda stood up and spoke about her ideas, all of which were right on target, and then Drea took the floor again. She went over her to-do lists and was just finishing up when Mason walked through the door, holding a poster board.

Their eyes met, and she froze inside. He smiled at her, a dazzler that revealed his dimples, then apologized to everyone for being late and interrupting. Mason took a place beside her at the front of the room, and the slight hint of his cologne immediately filled her personal space. Breathing it in jarred a memory of being naked with him, losing her inhibitions and giving herself so freely. My goodness, she'd never done anything as wildly erotic as making love to a man on a kitchen chair before. It had been thrilling. Her body heated at the memory and she reined herself in from the rampant thoughts totally unfit for the boardroom.

"It appears Mr. Boone has something to share with us, so I'll let him have the floor now."

Mason turned to her, but she couldn't bring herself to meet his eyes again for fear the entire boardroom

would see something she was dead set on concealing. She immediately took her seat.

"Thank you, Miss MacDonald."

She only half listened as he showed the volunteers
a detailed mock-up of the grounds at Rising Springs,
where everything would take place, from the pony
rides and game booths to the art auction and dinner. He was impressive, but she already knew that
firsthand.

When he was done with his presentation, he answered questions about the ranch and how it would
all work. The dream date raffle also drew enthusias-
tic praise from the group.

Once the meeting concluded, Drea made quick
work of gathering up her notes. When she heard
laughter coming from the other side of the room, she
looked up. Mason and Linda were chuckling about
something they thought dreadfully funny, and sudden sharp pangs stole into her heart. It wasn't easy
seeing the two of them smiling at each other, seeing
Linda's gleaming eyes fixed on Mason. It was obvious she thought the world of him.

Drea grabbed her briefcase and moved toward the
door.

"Drea, hang on a sec. I need to discuss something
with you," Mason called out in his deep baritone.

She turned to find both of them looking at her. "I'll
be in touch, Drea. Bye for now," Linda said, giving
her a little wave.

"Goodbye, Linda."

When the woman exited and closed the door behind her, Drea was left alone in the room with Mason. He walked over to her. "Where are you running off to?" he asked.

"I'm a little busy today," she said.

"Too busy to say hello?"

"Hello," she said softly.

He didn't find her joke funny. His eyes were on her, that dreamy, deep dark gaze latching on. He smelled delicious and looked even more so. She backed up a step.

"I've been thinking about you," he said. "How are you?"

"Fine. Busy, like I said," she blurted.

"Actually, I can't stop thinking about you. Have you been thinking about me, Drea?"

"No."

He gave her a crooked smile. "Liar."

Mason was so confident; he would never believe he hadn't left an impression. And she would have a difficult time denying it. "This isn't the place," she said, as forcefully as she could.

"Name the place, Drea. And I'll be there."

Oh God. No. No. "We can't, Mason. We said one night."

"Maybe we were wrong. Maybe we need more than one night."

His hand came up to her face and he stroked her cheek. His touch warmed everything cold inside and now she couldn't look away, couldn't stop staring at him. "Go away," she whispered.

"I can't," he said, stepping closer, cupping her face in his palm.

"I don't like you," she said, so quietly she could barely hear herself.

"I know. But you like the way I make you feel."

And he liked how she made him feel alive and vital again. Though he hadn't mentioned it since the very first kiss, she understood his attraction to her. He'd been dead inside, deeply grieving the loss of his family, a heartbroken man in pain. She'd been the one to wake him up to pleasure again, and of course he wanted more. His body was obviously craving life and lust again.

But could the same be true of her? Was having a satisfying sexual relationship good for her, too?

It sure felt that way when she was with him.

"Drea, you're thinking about it."

"I'm…not. I need to go."

He dropped his hand from her face and immediate disappointment set in. What was wrong with her? Deep down she understood this wouldn't end well, so shouldn't she be relieved that he let her go?

He was messing with her head, confusing her.

"You can't avoid me forever," he said.

"I know that. We've got a common work goal. It's important to remember that."

"I haven't forgotten the good we can do for the community." He focused on her mouth and then quickly swept his gaze over the rest of her body. It was enough to send shivers along her spine and quicken her pulse. "We're capable of separating the two, Drea."

"I'm not so sure of that." He had no idea what he was asking of her. He had no idea of her pain and suffering. She had too much pride to tell him what she'd gone through. She hadn't trusted anyone with her secret, and Mason was the last person on earth she'd tell.

"Maybe I'm sure enough for both of us."

She glanced at his mouth, recalling what those lips had done to her, how expertly he'd kissed her, and the memory caught her off guard. Her mask of indifference crumbled and she felt completely exposed.

"Drea, sweetheart." He took her hand and pulled gently until she was encircled in his arms, pressed against his chest. Then he kissed her thoroughly, devouring her lips as if he were starving. The kiss ended too quickly, yet both of them were completely breathless. Mason smiled at her, satisfaction in his expression as if to say he'd been right. They needed more time, more nights.

Maybe they did. Maybe Mason *was* right but it scared her and she had to end it now. "I'd better go." This was not what she'd expected when she'd come home to Boone Springs. Mason was changing all the rules and confusing her. It wasn't fair.

"I'll see you soon, Drea," Mason said confidently.

Oh no, he wouldn't. Not if she could help it.

"Dad, next time please ask me before you accept a dinner invitation from the Boones. I was planning on working late tonight." And the last person she wanted to see socially was Mason. They'd had their day and night, and now it was over, but she couldn't tell her father that.

Drea muttered under her breath as she and her father walked up the path to the Boone mansion. When she'd seen Mason as the hospital earlier, he didn't say a word about dinner, yet he must've known.

"I thought you'd want to spend more time with Lottie. Lord above, Drea. Can't I do anything right?"

Drea's shoulders fell. She had been hard on her dad for years, and she'd never accepted his *acceptance* of losing Thundering Hills to the Boones. Why hadn't he fought harder to save their home? "Yeah, Dad, you can. You do." He'd made a supreme effort to win her over since she'd been home. She shouldn't take out her bad mood on him. He had no idea what Mason had put her through, back then and…now.

She couldn't fault Mason for *now;* she took full responsibility for spending the night with him. It had been her own once-in-a-lifetime guilty pleasure, and now she was trying desperately, and without much success, to put that all behind her. "I'm just… Never mind."

"For what it's worth, I'm sorry…about everything," her dad said.

His tone was heart-wrenching.

She didn't mean to sound like a scrooge. And none of this was really his fault. It was hers, for caving in and letting Mason upend her life the way he had. "No, I'm sorry, Dad. I guess I'm stressed about the job. And yes, of course I want to spend time with Lottie. Let's just go and have a nice time tonight." She slipped her arm through his and smiled. "Okay?"

He hesitated a moment, then gave her a nod and a smile back. He seemed relieved and that was all she could ask for at the moment. "Sounds good to me."

Her father looked really nice tonight. He'd never had a smoother shave, his silvery hair was newly cut and tidy, and he'd put on a crisp button-down shirt and pair of slacks for the occasion. On his head was his ever present tan Stetson.

He rang the doorbell and a few moments later Lottie appeared, wearing an apron tied around her waist over a lovely rose silk blouse and skirt, her blond hair touching her shoulders. Drea heard a sudden noise: a quiet intake of breath from her father as he removed his hat.

"Welcome, you two," Lottie said, opening her arms to Drea. "You come here and let me give you a big hug."

Drea laughed and stepped forward, immediately cocooned in Lottie's brand of motherly love. She closed her eyes and hugged back. Only Lottie could make her feel this way, as if she was loved unconditionally. "So good to see you again, Lottie. You look wonderful."

"Thank you. Same here, sweetheart."

Her father remained stonily quiet.

"Hello, Drew."

"Lottie."

Drea wanted to roll her eyes at the two of them,

but whatever it was between them they'd have to work out on their own.

"Please come in. Everyone is here."

Lottie led them into the main drawing room, where all three Boone brothers were conversing. Lucas and Risk leaned against the river rock fireplace mantel, and Mason immediately stood up from his chair as they walked in.

His gaze latched on to her and she felt the burn from across the room. Suddenly all the intimate things they'd done to each other were up front and center in her mind. It was as if Mason owned her, at least a little bit, because of what they'd shared. How they'd been with each other.

But she'd had too many years of crushing on him as a young girl and then too many years of hating him as an adult. She was tired of being owned by Mason. Tired of letting him have that much power over her.

She aimed her greeting at Mason's brothers, the other culprits of the Boone clan.

"Hey, Drea," Lucas said, giving her a smile. He'd grown into a handsome man, with his military haircut and piercing eyes. Risk gave her a wave.

"Lucas. Risk." She wasn't exactly on friendly terms with them, but had to be cordial since she'd been invited to dine with them, and they'd be helping with the fund-raiser.

Lottie made a good effort to engage them all in conversation, the topic being fund-raising. It was a good ice-breaker; Drea could speak for hours on the subject. Mason chimed in, too, adding his insights as Lottie poured wine for everyone but Drew. She handed him a tall glass of iced tea.

Five minutes into their discussion, the doorbell rang. "We've given Jessica the night off, so please excuse me while I get the door," Lottie said.

A short time later, Lottie led Katie into the room. She held a big pastry box in her hands. "Look who was kind enough to deliver our dessert to us. I've invited her to stay for dinner, but I think Katie needs some arm-twisting."

Katie scanned the room, her gaze stopping for a heartbeat on Lucas. He put down his wineglass and faced her squarely, giving her a look that smoldered, before catching himself. Everyone else spoke up. Drea especially wanted her friend to stay. With Mason here, she could really use reinforcements. "Please join us, Katie."

She glanced at Drea's form-fitting black dress, silver jewelry and high heels. "I'm, ah, I don't think so," she said. Clearly, Katie thought she was out of place in her work clothes. "Thank you, though."

Katie had shoulder-length blond hair and the softest blue eyes, and she could wear a pair of jeans like nobody's business. More importantly, she was a good person, through and through.

Mason stepped up. "Why not stay and have a bite with us? We have a new foal in the stable you'd just about fall in love with. I'm sure Luke would love to show it to you."

Katie was a horse lover from way back and this

sparked a light in her gaze, though she avoided eye contact with Luke, staring at Mason instead.

"He's a beauty, too," Risk chimed in.

"Looks like the decision's made, Katie," Lottie said. "You're staying."

Katie forced a smile and nodded. "Okay, thank you. I would…love to."

Lottie took the box out of her hands and replaced it with a glass of wine. "Here you go. You all talk while I put these away and check on dinner."

"Want some help?" Drea's father asked Lottie.

Lottie's brows rose. She couldn't recall the last time Drew had offered her any help with anything. "Well now, that would be nice."

Lottie entered the kitchen, Drew a few steps behind her as she mulled over her confusing feelings. She'd known him forever, it seemed, but he'd always been Maria's guy.

He'd started off being a good provider for his family, a good father to young Drea and a pretty good husband to her best friend. But after tragedy struck, he'd simply given up…on everything. He'd let his ranch go to ruin, he'd stopped fathering Drea, and worst of all, he'd sought comfort in a bottle. How many years had he wasted? Lottie had promised Maria that she'd watch out for Drew and Drea when the time came. And she had, as much as she could without being a thorn in their sides. But Drew had been so dang hard to deal with. There was no reasoning with an alcoholic. Drew had had to come out of it on his own. He had, but not before causing a lot of damage.

Lottie put the cupcakes on the kitchen counter and turned to find Drew's soft green eyes on her.

"You look real nice tonight, Lottie."

"I bet it killed you to say that," she said, giving him a brief smile. There was truth to her words, but Lottie also had trouble accepting compliments from him. They were rare and made her uncomfortable.

"Well, no. It didn't, actually. That shade of pink suits you."

He looked good tonight, too, better than she'd seen him in a long while. "So do you. Look nice, I mean."

He cleared his throat and stared at her. When they weren't bickering, as they were prone to do, Lottie didn't know how to react. "Here, make yourself useful." She handed him a bowl of fresh greens.

"What's this?" He gave the dish a horrified look, as if weeds were growing inside it.

"Quinoa and kale salad."

Drew's face wrinkled up, but even that couldn't detract from his good looks. "Why?"

She laughed. He was so predictable. She knew he'd rebel against her nourishing meal. "So you can get used to eating healthy foods."

"Oh, the devil. Mason said you might try to change my eating habits. What else do you have planned for supper?"

"All good things, I assure you."

"That's what I'm afraid of. You got dressing for this *salad*?"

"Yep, right here. Lemon vinaigrette."

She handed him the carafe and their fingers brushed.

His gaze shot to hers and she paused for a second, taken by unfamiliar sensations of warmth. She didn't know where to stash those feelings. And Drew wouldn't stop staring at her, the moment seemingly suspended in time. Finally, she snapped out of it. "You go on, bring in the salad. I'll get the rolls."

"Rolls? Now we're talking," he said eagerly.

"Don't get too excited. They're gluten free."

As he marched out of the kitchen, Drew muttered something about how a man could starve to death from good intentions. Lottie braced her hands on the edge of the counter and smiled. She was trying to do right by Drea and Maria, and Drew giving her grief about it wasn't unexpected.

What was unexpected was how much she enjoyed ringing his bell.

Six

Drea finished her meal. She had to admit the dinner hadn't been uncomfortable at all. Lottie had made sure of it. She could talk endlessly about her adventures. She'd traveled the world, and had led a really intriguing life. The woman wasn't the least bit shy about telling everyone about the ups and downs of living large. The one thing she didn't have was a husband and children of her own. Oddly, she'd never married. Drea had always thought the Boones were Lottie's fill-in family. Whenever she decided to stop and rest up a spell before heading out again, she'd spend time with her nephews. Lord knew, the boys loved and respected her to pieces.

"Mason, you haven't touched your broccoli." Lottie narrowed her eyes at him.

"You know I'm not a fan, Aunt."

"And Risk, that poached chicken isn't going to eat itself."

"Yes, ma'am," Risk said, eyeing his brothers for mercy.

"And—"

"I had a late lunch, Aunt Lottie." Lucas rubbed his stomach. "I'm about to bust."

Lottie pursed her lips. The boys were not helping her cause in the least and Drea wasn't going to let her go down without a fight, especially since her father had a big smug smile on his face. All the woman was trying to do was to get her dad to eat a healthier diet. Apparently, none of her nephews were in her corner.

"Lottie, this is a wonderful meal. I think I'll have seconds," Drea said, and right away Mason lifted the dish of chicken and passed it to her. His smirk was nothing short of daring. "Thank you," she said, tipping up her chin as she helped herself to another piece.

"Me, too," Katie said. "I love how you made the salad, Lottie. It's light and delicious."

Lottie nodded at Drew before passing over the salad bowl. "Here you go, Katie. I can tell you girls have a good palate."

Drea's father put his head down, concealing his amusement. Well, at least Lottie could make him smile. It was a good distraction from having to deal with Mason.

His eyes were forever on her and it rattled her nerves. As much as she was at ease during dinner, thanks to Lottie, every time she stole a glance at Mason he was watching her. Not only did his eyes burn straight through to her unguarded heart, he looked devastatingly handsome tonight in a pair of dark pants and a caramel-brown snap-down shirt. What was under that shirt made her head spin; she was reminded of the ripped chest with just enough wisps of hair to weave her fingers through as she'd kissed the hot skin there. His face was chiseled perfection, made even sexier by the dark stubble on his jaw.

Why did he have to appeal to her so much? Why couldn't she forget about the night they'd shared? She'd promised herself it would be only that. *One night.* She wasn't foolish enough to think that she could totally forgive Mason and his family, or to believe that he was over the loss of his wife.

They'd agreed on one night and now Mason wasn't playing fair. He wasn't letting it be. He was pursuing her, and Lord, if all he had to do was aim some scorching looks her way to get her to rethink her resolve, she was in deep trouble.

"How about you all take a look at that adorable new colt in the stable," Lottie said. "I'll get some coffee brewing and set out Katie's scrumptious cupcakes."

Katie rose. "I'll help you, Lottie."

"Don't be silly. You need to see that colt. Luke, take Katie on up to the stable, will you?"

Luke tossed his napkin onto the table and rose. "Okay, sure. Katie?"

Her friend's tight smile only confirmed to Drea that she didn't want to be alone with Luke. He'd been engaged to Shelly, Katie's older sister, and had walked out on her right before their wedding. He'd joined the Marines and had been gone a while, but Katie's family still hadn't forgiven him. "Will the rest of you be joining us?" Katie asked.

"I'd like to see it," Drea said, coming to her friend's aid. Katie and Luke had once been easy friends. Now things were strained between them.

"I'll stay behind," Risk said. "I've already seen the colt."

"I think I'll just sit a spell on the porch, if you all don't mind," her father said.

Mason didn't say a word, but as Luke ushered Katie out the door, Mason waited for Drea on the threshold. "Haven't you seen the colt?" she asked him.

"Not since Trinket gave birth."

He gestured for her to exit, and when she did, he followed. She did her best to catch up with Luke and Katie, and she was making ground until Mason took her hand from behind, slowing her down.

"Let the two of them talk," he said quietly. "I think Luke needs to repair some of the damage."

She stopped and looked at him. "You think Lucas can do that?"

"He can try. They were pretty close friends."

"Yeah, well. Things change. People change. I'm not sure Katie wants to be alone with Luke."

"What you really mean is you don't want to be alone with me. Isn't that right?"

She sighed and all the fight went out of her. "Maybe."

"Why?"

"You know why! We made a deal and now you're going back on it."

Once Luke and Katie were way up ahead, Drea and Mason began slowly walking toward the stable. "I just think the deal was a mistake."

"Taking that trip to Los Angeles together was the mistake," she said.

"It's killing you that you're starting to like me."

"I don't…like you."

Mason grinned. Oh, he was infuriating. He had enough confidence to fill up a football stadium. Normally, she liked that trait in a man. She'd never been attracted to weak-kneed men who were wishy-washy about themselves. Mason seemed so sure of everything, except when it came to his own heart. He'd been broken, and he was just coming out of that. He was starting to rebuild himself again, but she had no place in his life. Correction: she wanted no place in his life.

When they were in LA, it had all seemed so easy. They were far away from Texas, away from family and friends, away from reality, sharing the night on a beautiful beach. It had almost been as if she were a different woman and Mason a different man. She'd fully expected things to get back to normal once they'd touched down on Texas soil again.

"You don't like me, even a little?"

"Well, maybe I see some redeeming qualities in you." She was being honest.

"Like what? I'm curious."

"You're decisive. You get things done. I admire that."

He nodded. "Anything else?"

"Well…" She stared at him for a long moment. The sun was setting, and only a glimmer of light touched his face now. "You're good—"

"In bed?" He was smiling, and those hidden dimples popped out underneath his sexy day-old beard.

She shook her head. "You have a tremendous…"

His brows lifted wickedly.

"Ego."

"I thought you were going to say—"

"Mason," she warned. "Don't."

"We had a good time in LA."

"It's going nowhere."

"Do you want it to go somewhere?" he asked.

"Of course not. But I can't forget certain things."

"I can't forget certain things, either. Like the way you tremble when I touch you. Or the way your body responds to mine, or the feel of your silky hair or—"

"Mason, please…that's not what I meant."

They reached the stable and Mason glanced inside. "Let's give the two of them some privacy." He took her hand and tugged her toward the back of the structure. She followed his lead, not putting up any resistance. Why didn't she? She had no answer to that question. She could've just as easily held her ground and walked inside the building to meet up with Katie and Lucas.

Now her back was to the wall, literally, and Mason's big body blocked her vision of anything else. All she saw was one gorgeous man, staring at her like she held the answers to the universe in the palm of her hand. "What are you doing?" *To me?* she really wanted to ask.

"I'm spending time with you. I've thought about little else these past few days."

She had to admit that Mason was getting to her. What she liked about him was his determination to never give up. But that trait could also be her downfall.

"I'm leaving when the fund-raiser is over."

He lifted a strand of her long hair and twirled it around his finger. "It's not like we both don't know that, sweetheart."

Sweetheart. There it was again. She wasn't his sweet anything. She really wasn't, but his soft tone made her think otherwise. And it confused her to no end. "This isn't good."

"You're right. It isn't good. It's pretty great."

He leaned in, his face coming inches from hers, his mouth, that delectable expert mouth, so close.

"I—I make you…feel things," she stuttered.

His lips lifted in a smile. "So true."

"That's all this is."

"I make you feel things, too," he whispered, cradling her face in his hands. "Tell me it's not so and I'll back off, Drea."

She opened her mouth to deny it. To deny him. But the words wouldn't come. What was wrong with her? Why couldn't she say no to him and mean it? The look on his face, the hunger in his eyes spoke to her. He smelled of lime and musk, something expensive and rare that was drawing her to him, making her want, making her crave. All she could do was feel his approach, leaning closer until his hips touched hers and her breasts were crushed against his chest.

Memories flooded in. Of unparalleled kisses. Of being naked with him. Of their two bodies completely in sync with each other. A whimper escaped her mouth as she surrendered totally.

And then his lips were on hers, his mouth taking claim, his kiss a beautiful reminder of how much she'd missed…this. Not *him*. She wasn't missing him so much as she missed the womanly way he made her feel. Desirable and attractive. She had his total approval and that was something she hadn't often felt while growing up. To be honest, her adult life hadn't been all that glorious, either. So naturally, she would take what Mason offered. That had to be it. That had to be the reason his kisses made her legs weak and her heart flutter wildly.

At least that's what she told herself as Mason's mouth demanded more of her, as his body went rigid. It was heady knowing she made him come alive. A true boost to her morale, she had to admit.

As he pressed his hard body home, her lips parted in a moan of pure delight. Everything tingled. Every sensation was heightened.

Voices and then footsteps reached her ears. "Oh no," she whispered.

"Shush." Mason kissed her quiet.

Lucas and Katie were leaving the stable and heading back to the house. It was dark now. Drea and Mason stood still and waited until the sound of their footsteps receded.

"We need to go back," she whispered. An owl hooted and leaves of surrounding trees rustled in the night breeze. The fall air grew crisp but Drea's body was still heated, her heart still raced.

Mason released a deep sigh. A houseful of people waited for them and they couldn't do this any longer. He took her hand. "Let's go see the foal for a minute," he said.

"Okay, yes. We should." So that they could say they had. So that no one would get suspicious.

Once in the stable, they watched mama with her new babe. It was a thing of beauty and grace, and Drea was struck by deep yearning. Remembering her loss, the child she would never know, only compounded the feeling.

Mason stared into the paddock filled with a layer of straw to cushion the horses from the wooden walls and hard ground. Drea had grown up on a ranch, too, and welcomed the pungent scents, the smell of leather and earth.

"Meet me later tonight," he said, his voice firm, determined.

She squeezed her eyes closed. Not because it was

a ridiculous idea, but because it was an enticing one. "I...can't."

Mason turned to her and his eyes spoke of promises he would fulfill.

Her body still hummed from his kisses. He wanted more. So did she. But it was impossible.

"Why can't you?" he asked. "And I'd like the truth."

She drew breath into her lungs. "Aside from the obvious reasons—"

"Like you hate me for hurting you, for taking away your family land? You blame me for all the woes of the world?"

"Mason."

He pressed closer to her. Wrapping his hand around her neck, he pulled her in and kissed her thoroughly, without pause, softening up all her hard, unsettled edges.

"Now tell me the truth," he whispered over her lips.

"Where would we meet? I mean, you live here, and it's not exactly private. And my dad's place is off-limits."

Perhaps she'd revealed too much of her thoughts. She should be denying him this, outright refusing his suggestion. But she couldn't. Maybe she wanted to see what he had in mind. Maybe she was more than a little bit intrigued by a secret rendezvous.

Mason stroked a finger across her cheek, his tender touch creating tingles down to her toes. "At The Baron. I keep a room there, for when I work in town."

"Your hotel?"

He nodded. "I'll be there at eleven. Waiting for you."

A dozen questions filled her head. She wasn't a teenager, sneaking out for a date. She wasn't a woman who liked lying. But she'd have to do one or the other in order to meet Mason.

"I don't know."

"Think about it, sweetheart. And you do know. You just can't face it yet."

Face what? That she wanted him? That after their time in LA she'd been thinking about Mason in a purely unbusinesslike way.

So much for *Business with Mason*. That had lasted as long as a snowball in hell.

He kissed her again, then took her hand and led her out of the stable.

Already she felt like a fraud, entering the Boone home pretending that nothing monumental was happening between them. Pretending that they weren't crazily attracted to each other.

Back at the house, Katie pulled her into the kitchen as the others were drinking coffee. Her friend whispered, "What happened to you two out there?"

"You mean, when we didn't show in the stable?"

"Yes, that's what I mean. You were supposed to be my cover. I didn't want to be alone with Lucas."

"I know. Sorry. I let you down. Was it horrible?"

"What? No, not really. We're just distant friends now, is all."

"Okay, good. That's what I was hoping. But he was sort of ogling you at dinner tonight."

Katie giggled. "I was just going to say the same thing about Mason. He wasn't letting up. His eyes were all for you. So, what happened out behind the stable tonight?"

Drea gasped, partly in shock. Not about Katie knowing something was going on, but the idea that maybe the others were piecing things together, as well. "You know?"

"I don't think Luke gave it a thought, but I figured something was up."

"It's complicated," Drea said, keeping her voice down. "I can't go into detail, but something happened between me and Mason when we were in LA and now he wants to see me again. Like, later tonight."

"Go."

Drea blinked. "What do you mean, go?"

"Drea, you haven't been with a man in a long while. And maybe…well, maybe you just need to get Mason out of your system. Geesh, I sound like a guy, don't I? But it's true. How can you move on with your life until this part of it is satisfied? See what happens with Mason. I mean, if you didn't want to meet him, if you thought it ridiculous, you wouldn't have told me. You would've shot him down immediately. But you didn't do that. You want to go."

"I don't like sneaking around."

"Sounds kind of exciting, if you ask me." Katie's voice got animated, making Drea smile and shake her head.

Her decision now made, she gave Katie her best

stern look. "If this goes south, I'll come after you, Katie girl."

Her friend kissed her cheek. "Go, and have a good time on my behalf. Heaven knows, I've been a safe little mouse all my life, so at least let me enjoy a bit of intrigue through my bestie."

"So glad I'm a source of your entertainment."

Katie shoved a bunch of extra napkins into Drea's hands while she grabbed the plate of cupcakes, "Come on, let's get back out there before someone comes looking for us."

"Yeah, Luke might come searching for you."

"That would be a no-can-ever-do," Katie said.

"Yeah, and that's what I thought about Mason Boone for all of my grown-up life. Just goes to show, never say never."

Drea stood outside the door of The Baron Hotel's top floor suite, ready to knock. That she was here at all still shocked the stuffing out of her. But Katie had been right. Drea had unfinished business to settle with Mason and so his proposed midnight interlude might not go exactly as he'd planned.

Getting away hadn't been hard at all. She'd waited until her father was sawing logs, before quietly stepping out of the house. She'd left him a note saying that she had trouble sleeping and had gone for a drive, just in case he woke and didn't find her home. All that was true, so she hadn't really lied. At least that was what she told herself.

She knocked on the door softly and heard footsteps approach.

Swallowing hard, she braced herself. When Mason opened the door, his shoulders relaxed, a small smile surfaced and she read great relief in his expression. This wasn't the confident man she'd expected to find. Instead, Mason's vulnerability had shone through, touching something deep and precious in her heart. He hadn't been sure she'd show up. And he'd been worried, perhaps even saddened, to think she'd let him down.

It wasn't fair. She had Mason pegged as an arrogant pain in her side, and he was proving her wrong.

"Drea." There was a wistful tone in his voice. So different than the man who ran an empire, the man who commanded respect at all times. Mason Boone was full of surprises.

"I'm...here." She lifted her shoulders, then let them fall.

He took her hand and gently pulled her into the room. "I'm happy to see that."

He let her hand go and she walked into the suite taking in the living area, with its fireplace and twin sofas facing each other, the dining area and the hallway that led to the other rooms. It was luxurious and grand, something she'd expect from a Boone. But it was also homey in a way that said Mason spent a lot of time here, from the scattering of square, embroidered pillows on the floor, to the sports magazines on the coffee table to a giant screen TV on the wall. She recognized the pillows as being Lottie's handiwork. Peaches, oranges and apples filled a bowl on the kitchen counter and photos of Rising Springs Ranch graced the hallway walls. Soft classical music played in the background, perhaps the biggest surprise of all.

"Is this your Zen place?" she asked turning to find him watching her from the middle of the living room.

"Or my man cave."

His gaze was forever on her, as if to say he couldn't believe she was really here.

"No, it's definitely Zen." She walked to the window and stared out at the town Mason's ancestors had established. How must that feel? To know your family had built this town from the ground up. To have streets, a hospital, an entire town named after the Boones. To have that entitlement.

She looked at Mason, standing there, curiosity on his beautiful face. "You didn't think I'd come, did you?"

He sighed and walked over to her. "I'm…a little surprised."

"No one is more surprised than me, Mason."

He stood at arm's length from her and his presence consumed her. He was that type of man, one who could overpower with just one glance. Usually he loomed large, but tonight she was seeing a different side of him. "Do you still resent me and all the Boones?"

"My feelings about you are…complicated."

He stepped closer and entwined his fingers with

hers. "Can we try to uncomplicate things? Can we just talk about it, Drea? About that night so long ago?"

His question made her jittery. She wanted to yank her hand away, to turn her back on him, to walk out the door if necessary. She'd lost her baby and a big part of herself, after all. How could she possibly explain the damage that was done after that night? She'd struggled for years with all of it.

But as Katie had said, she needed to be able to get on with her life. To move past this. And maybe there was no better way than to talk it through. "At one point in my life, you were my everything, Mason." God, it was hard to admit that.

"Come here," he said, leading her to the sofa. She sank down and he sat beside her. They faced each other, still holding hands. "You were saying?"

"You heard what I said. I was halfway in love with you, Mason."

"And I shouldn't have let it go that far. I was attracted to you. I'd always liked you. We used to play together, if you remember."

"Of course I remember. We were friends once."

"And then, when you were bucked from your horse and took a hard fall, I found you in the meadow. Your ankle was bruised and you couldn't put any pressure on it."

"You were wonderful that day," she said, remembering how gallant he'd been. He'd stayed with her, helping remove her shoe and using a cold can of soda pop he'd been drinking to keep the swelling down on her ankle. He'd missed a baseball game with his friends to stay with her. And then, when she was able to stand up, he'd lifted her and carried her to an old carriage house on their property. The chemistry between them had been off the charts. She'd never looked at Mason that way before, but having him tend her, having his dark concerned eyes on her, having him touch and care for her, had made her dizzy. From that moment on, she'd set her sights on him.

"And you were seventeen."

"A month away from my eighteenth birthday, Mason. I wasn't a kid."

"I didn't think so, either. But you were a virgin and I was going for my final semester at Texas A&M."

"I was willing, Mason. That night, up in your bedroom. We were all alone."

He heaved a big sigh. "I know. It was so hard to say no to you. But I had to. You were Drew's daughter, for one. And he was a family friend, even if you didn't want to think so at the time."

"But we'd been seeing each other every day for a full month and I knew my heart. I told you I was ready."

"Look at me, Drea," he commanded, and she lifted her chin to meet his gaze. "You also said one other thing to me. Do you remember what that was?"

She thought back and couldn't really recall what else she'd said. For all these years, she'd blocked out the hurtful memory of that night, the exact words spoken, but the humiliation had lingered on. She shook her head. "No."

He squeezed her hand gently. "You said…you needed me. Not wanted, not loved, but needed me."

She pulled back, wrenching her hand from his in utter shock. "Oh, so you thought I was this needy kid, starving for affection. You thought you'd get stuck with me, the pathetic daughter of a widower drunk, a girl so confused about her feelings that she'd give up her virginity to you. What you did to me that night was cruel."

Tears stung her eyes. This was horrific. She didn't think she could ever be more humiliated than when she'd bared her body to Mason and he'd rejected her. But this was just as bad, if not worse.

"No, that's not what I'm saying." Mason's voice sharpened immediately. "I wanted you, Drea. But there were too many obstacles blocking us and I had to be the grown-up. I had to deny you and myself. It was for the best. And I'm sorry that I hurt you, but I had to be firm. I had to make sure not to leave any doubt in your mind, because…because there was doubt in mine. So yes, I spoke harshly to you and I've regretted it every day since. But we did the right thing, Drea. We did."

She got up and walked to the window, staring at the lights of the town. "You wanted me to hate you. Well, you succeeded. You have no idea what your rejection did to me."

Mason came up behind her. "I did what I thought best for you at the time. I cared about you too much to use you, to have you for one night and then take off. My conscience wouldn't allow it, but no, I didn't want you to hate me."

"But I did. Especially after what your family had already done to mine. I thought you heartless and mean, and wondered if I'd ever meant anything to you."

"Drea, listen to me. The Boones aren't as bad as you seem to think. We're not greedy robber barons after people's land. My family tried to help yours."

He wasn't convincing her.

Mason clasped her shoulders, his hands gentle, as if testing to see if she'd flinch. But his touch, like always, comforted her instead, giving her solace and peace. She'd spent so much time hating him that now there wasn't much hatred left. Only regret. She had so many regrets.

"If it's any consolation to you, I didn't date for nearly a year after that. Every time I looked at a woman, I thought of you. I swear it, Drea. It's hard to admit, but I have second-guessed that night in my head many times."

If she could believe him, it helped knowing that he'd suffered a little bit, too. That he'd had doubts about letting her go. It helped her ego and her pride and also helped put things in perspective. She'd never heard his side of the story before. She'd never known his motivation for breaking things off and breaking her heart.

Yet there was more to her story, but she couldn't reveal it to him. It would only serve to prove he'd been right. She had been needy, a girl craving love and affection.

She'd done a stupid thing and maybe now she could put the past behind her. Her hatred depleted, maybe now she could move on with her life, just like Katie had said. For the first time in a long time, she would be free of that burden. Her feelings about the Boones in general were a different story. Her resentment about Thundering Hills was still there, but no longer was she driven by contempt and anger. "It does help knowing that."

Mason kissed the back of her neck, then nibbled along her collarbone. She arched her head, giving him more access. The skin where he kissed her burned.

"If you want to leave, I'd understand. But I don't want you to, sweetheart. I want you to stay."

She turned around and he immediately wrapped her in his arms. His head came down and his lips brushed hers gently, sweetly. Mason pulled back and smiled at her, and there was that vulnerability in his eyes again. When he was like that, she was even more attracted to him. The look on his face as he waited for her answer had her melting inside.

"I want to stay."

A wide grin spread across his face. He squeezed her tightly and kissed her again, but briefly. "Would you like something to drink? Eat?"

"After eating Katie's Molten Ganache cupcake, I don't think I'll ever eat again. But I would like a drink."

"A drink it is. What can I get you?"

"White wine?"

He nodded and headed toward the kitchen. "Have a seat. I'll get it for you."

She settled on the sofa, and while she waited, made note of the fact that Mason didn't have one photo of his wife in any of the rooms she'd been in. No wedding pictures, no pictures of the two of them lounging around, riding horses or sitting on a fence at Rising Springs Ranch.

Were the memories too hard for him?

She'd heard people say Larissa was the love of his life. He'd been crushed when she died.

Yet Mason almost never brought her up.

And so now here Drea was, hardly a replacement for his dead wife. No, she was a brief interlude, and she had to remember that. After the fund-raiser, she'd head home to her pretty, cool apartment and life in New York, and Mason would move on, too.

"Here you go," he said, handing her a glass of wine. He sat down beside her with his own drink, something golden-brown, bourbon probably.

"Thank you." She sipped her drink and breathed in Mason. She should never mix alcohol and the scent of a gorgeous man. Or maybe she should. She smiled.

"What's going on in your head?"

"Nothing."

She took another sip.

"You smiled. What were you thinking?"

"Okay," she said. "I'm thinking that I'm here with you without…"

"Without hating me?"

She nodded.

"So you like me now?"

"Well," she said, bringing the glass to her mouth. "Let's not go that far."

There was a gleam in Mason's eyes. He wasn't vulnerable anymore, far from it. His expression meant danger and pleasure and promise.

He took the glass out of her hand and set it down. "Actually, let's go as far as we can tonight," he whispered. He took a last gulp of alcohol and then kissed her hard on the lips.

Her body reacted to the potent taste of whiskey, to the scent, the kiss, the man.

"You look amazing. I wanted to tell you earlier. That dress is—"

"Coming off?" She loved the look the surprise on his face.

He chuckled deep in his throat. "That, too, but it's gorgeous on you."

And five minutes later, after skillfully undressing each other, piece by piece, kiss after kiss, Mason lifted her up in his arms and carried her to the bedroom.

The bedroom was low-key but luxurious, with large dark furnishings. The windows looked out over the other side of town, toward the quiet suburbs of Boone Springs. The drapes were pulled back, and the light of the half-moon filtered in through nearly sheer curtains, splashing over Mason's body as he lowered her onto the bed. She felt the cool, silky sheets on her back.

Mason stared at her a moment, something dark flickering in his eyes before he joined her on the bed. That look frightened her. Was it guilt? Or doubt? Was he second-guessing all this? Had he lost his desire for her? "What?" she asked softly.

He didn't hesitate. "I'm thinking how beautiful you are."

His words sent a thrill through her body. Yet she had never wanted this. To be his experiment, to have him want her solely due to a crazy chemical attraction he had for her. But here she was, also lured by that undeniable chemistry, waiting and wanting to be dazzled by him again. It would all be okay as long as she recognized this for what it was. As long as she didn't let him in, the way she had as a teen.

"But are you okay with all of this?" he asked her.

"He asks as I'm naked in bed with him."

"Just making sure, sweetheart."

His next kiss wiped away any doubt.

Mason was a thorough lover, from his mind-numbing kisses to his attention to her body. He caressed her lovingly, gently massaging her breasts until her nipples ripened to tiny hard pebbles. His tongue did wonderful things, making her whimper in a way that couldn't be mistaken for anything other than pure sexual pleasure.

Her skin prickled as sizzling, sweeping heat poured into every crevice, and when he paid deep attention to the sweet spot below her navel, she cried out. His mouth was relentless, his hands were masterful. Her back arched off the bed as an earth-shattering release tore through her. She panted his name.

"I'm right here, darlin'."

And he *was* right there, now sheathed with protection and rolling onto his back so he lay next to her. She was still coming down from her high and Mason waited for her patiently.

Then he whispered, "Come to me, Drea."

He guided her so that she was on top, her legs straddling him. He circled her waist with his big hands and helped her, fitting her body to his. She sank onto him and her eyes shuttered closed. It was a beautiful joining.

"You are incredible like this." His voice was a husky mixture of awe and gratitude. "Your hair, your skin. You feel like heaven, Drea."

His words brought her joy. And her skin prickled again, the heat from before magnified. She didn't wait for him to move, but began a slow, steady gyration, sinking farther down, giving Mason a reason to grit his teeth and groan.

He touched her all over, his thumbs flicking across her breasts, his hand working magic below her waist. She sped up her pace, cementing that look of awe on his face. Her second release was intense, stronger than before, her voice at a higher pitch as she called out Mason's name.

Her completion couldn't be compared to anything she'd experienced before. Not that she was an expert. She'd had exactly three relationships in her life, and yes, Mason topped them all. But if she'd had a hundred, he would still come out the winner. She knew that for a fact.

She fell into his arms and he kissed her silly. And then he rolled them both over, so that he towered above her on the bed. She gazed up into his handsome face filled with hunger and lust.

"I want you, Mason," she said softly.

"You've got me," he said.

Then he drove his point home, telling her yes, indeed, she had him.

Mason's phone alarm woke him from a deep sleep. Normally, he liked waking up to Larissa's favorite song, Faith Hill's "Breathe." It was a humbling reminder of his wife, and the child he'd never know, and somehow it made him feel closer to them. He'd never thought to change it. If he did, it would be like losing another piece of Larissa. Another soul-emptying piece of her.

But today, he shut off the alarm quickly and hinged up to a sitting position.

"Hell." He ran his hand down his face. He didn't have to see the empty place beside him on the bed or look around the suite to know that Drea was gone. He should've been more considerate. He shouldn't have fallen asleep. At the very least he wanted to make sure she'd gotten home safely last night.

He would have gladly driven her home. He would've kissed her goodbye in the wee hours of the night and watched as she entered the cottage.

He rose and dressed then wandered over to the

window. Boone Springs was just rising, too, and the autumn sun was warming everything up.

He craved a cup of coffee to clear his head. Right now, his thoughts were on two women.

His wife, for one. Dead and buried two years ago next week. He didn't need a calendar under his nose to remember the date. He still saw her pretty face and the silky cinnamon hair that bounced off her shoulders when she walked. And those light blue eyes that lit like fireworks every time he smiled at her.

She'd moved to Boone Springs seven years ago, and he'd met her at his friend Trace Burrows's wedding. She'd been a college friend of the bride, just visiting town and looking for work. Mason had fallen hard for her immediately and was desperate for her to stay on in Boone Springs. Without her knowing it, he'd pulled some strings and she'd been hired as a television anchor for the local news station, WBN. She'd been great on camera and off.

After they were married, he'd fessed up about his desperation to keep her in town, hoping she wouldn't go ballistic. She'd only smiled. "I would've gotten the job without your help. I nailed that audition." That was Larissa. She'd been fierce and smart and wonderful.

Mason grabbed his phone and walked into the kitchen. He set up the coffeemaker to brew. Later, at the ranch, he'd get breakfast. For now, the steady drip, drip, drip of dark roast was enough to satisfy him.

That's when something shimmery on the hardwood floor caught his eye. He walked over and bent to pick it up. It was a long strand of looped silver, the necklace Drea had worn last night. As he stared at it, memories rushed in, of him removing her black dress, taking off her shoes and every other pretty little thing she wore. Man, he'd wanted her so badly last night.

He'd been struck that she'd shown up at all. And that they'd finally cleared the air about their past.

That's when his doubts had rushed in. He'd had a moment, a panic attack of emotion. Drea's resentment about him and his family had always been misguided, yet it had provided protection he could count on, a barrier she wouldn't allow to be broken. Because he was never going to fall in love again. He'd never have another permanent relationship. His wife was still in his heart.

"So now what, idiot?" he murmured, holding Drea's necklace in his hand. It was warm, like her. And sleek and beautiful. Also like her.

Mason picked up his phone and texted Drea. I have something of yours.

He waited a minute, poured his coffee and then received her answer. Did I lose my panties?

He laughed so hard coffee sloshed from his cup, just missing his hand. If you had, I wouldn't be giving them back.

Ha! What then?

Wait and see. I'll bring it by your place this morning.

I'll be at Katie's Kupcakes.

Great, save one for me. I'll see you there.

Mason put away his phone before she could text him not to come over. He was going to see her. To tell her he'd wanted to take her home last night. Any man of honor would do the same.

And that's where it got confusing. Because he had a sinking feeling that even if she hadn't lost her necklace and slipped out of his place quietly last night, he would've found a reason to see her again today.

Seven

Drea didn't have to try another cupcake. She'd chosen her favorite and that was that. When she set her sights on something, usually there was no changing her mind. "This one, Katie. This has got to be one of them."

In the back work area of the bakery, Drea leaned over the stainless-steel countertop and took another big lick of raspberry cream cheese frosting. The cupcake was so pretty, a lemon rosemary cake infused with raspberry filling and covered with delicious icing. "I love your idea, by the way."

Katie had offered to come up with two signature cupcakes for the fund-raiser, one that appealed to adults and one for the kids. Of course, her other cupcakes would be for sale, too, and Katie was donating all the proceeds she earned to the cause. She was also overseeing the cupcake decorating booth.

"Thanks. And I agree. I love the combination of flavors in this one. So now we've got one for the adults. What about the kids?"

"Kids love all cupcakes." Drea continued to devour hers.

Great sex had a way of making her hungry. Her heart sped as she thought about the incredible night she'd shared with Mason. After he'd fallen asleep, she'd quickly dressed and driven home, making as little noise as possible as she entered the cottage. Luckily, her father had been sound asleep. She'd tiptoed to her room, undressed quietly and gotten into bed.

Sleep hadn't come easily. She'd missed Mason, missed waking up with him like she had at the beach house, breathing in his after-sex scent and snuggling up tight. But it was best this way. At least she didn't have to answer questions from her dad. That would've been awkward for sure.

"I want to make it special for the kids—a cupcake they can't pass up," Katie said.

Drea tapped a finger to her lips. "Well, what do kids love more than anything?"

"Christmas?"

She laughed. "So true, but not Christmas this time. I know…they love parties. Can you conjure up a party cupcake?"

"Confetti cake isn't new."

"No, but what about…a rainbow cupcake?"

Katie's eyes widened, and Drea could just see the

wheels of invention turning in her head. "I think I can do that. We'll have three flavors on the inside, and then I'll do a rainbow frosting on top. I don't know a single child who doesn't like rainbows."

"That sounds wonderful," Drea admitted, but then as an afterthought said, "But isn't it a lot of work?"

Katie grinned. "Not if you're helping me."

"Are you serious? I can't…bake. I'm so not a baker, and definitely not one of your caliber."

"You are a baker. It's not that hard. But I was teasing. I'll get extra help from Lori, my assistant, and it'll all work out. Besides, you'll be running the entire show at Rising Springs. You're gonna have your hands full that weekend."

"I know. It's hard to believe it's less than two weeks away."

"I'm looking forward to having the kids learn how to frost a cupcake. I've got all these ideas for decorating. Some moms and dads from Park Avenue Elementary School are going to run the booth with me."

"I think that's going to be a hit. Kids love that sort of thing."

The overhead bell on the shop door chimed. Katie took a peek out front. "Speaking of having your hands full. There's a gorgeous hunk of a guy out there, and I don't think he wants a cupcake."

"Mason?"

Katie nodded. "He looks impatient. He must be dying to see you."

"Don't be silly. He's only returning something of mine."

"That you left at his place last night?"

Drea opened her mouth, but nothing came out. She straightened out her dress, slipped her feet back into her heels and fluffed her hair a bit.

"You look great. Go. And remember, I want deets later. You owe me."

"Okay," she answered breathlessly.

She walked into the café, coming around the corner of the glass display case to face Mason. "Hi."

His eyes filled with warmth. She tried not to notice, not to make a big deal of the way he was looking at her. But her heart swelled and she was absolutely certain she was eyeing him with that very same look.

"Hi." His voice was husky and deep. He wore a tan shirt under an ink-black suit, no tie, his collar open at the throat. He removed his hat, smiled and then gave her a kiss on the cheek. "You ran out on me last night."

"Shh," she said, glancing out the window. It was midmorning and the bakery café was empty yet someone could walk in at any moment. "I didn't run out. You knew I had to get home before I turned into a pumpkin."

"Well then, Cinderella, I came to see if this fits." He dug into his pocket and came up with her silver loop necklace.

She smiled. "Not exactly a glass slipper."

"And I'm hardly a prince. But let's see if it fits."

Mason walked behind her, his body so close, his memorable scent teasing her nostrils. He lifted her ponytail out of the way, and his warm breath caressed the back of her neck. "You're trembling," he said as he secured the clasp.

"It's a little cold in here." It wasn't.

He nibbled on her nape, planting delicious kisses behind her ear. Her breathing hitched and she felt a hot tingling in her belly. "I can keep you warm."

"I know." Heat flushed her cheeks. She didn't often blush, but Mason was capable of bringing out new sides of her personality.

When he came around to face her, he noticed her pink cheeks, which should've embarrassed her. But there was an incredible softness in his eyes. Then he glanced at the necklace and his brows furrowed, his expression turning serious. "I would've driven you home last night."

"I had my car."

"Still, I should've made sure you got safely home."

"Thank you. But I didn't want to wake you."

"I missed you when I woke up."

Her breath caught in her throat. She didn't have a response for him. He was too devastatingly handsome and honest for her peace of mind. She'd felt the same way; leaving him asleep in his bed had made her feel terribly lonely. She hadn't felt that way in a long time.

When she didn't reply, he sighed. "What are you doing for lunch?"

"Lunch? I'm working through lunch. In case you don't realize it, the fund-raiser is less than two weeks away."

"And look at all the progress we've made. It's all gonna come together. Linda is working her buns off on promo for The Band Blue and the date with Sean. You've got a handle on the art auction. I heard you managed to get donations from several art galleries. That's huge."

"Yes, I'm excited about that. More than twenty-five paintings and five bronze sculptures, and some wood sculptures, as well. It should bring in a good deal of revenue. Is everything going well at the ranch?"

"Yeah, but I need your advice. There's things we need to go over."

"I'm happy to. When?"

"We can discuss it over lunch." His eyes twinkled. He'd caught her and all she could do was smile.

"You are persistent."

"It's for the cause, Drea. We both have to eat. Can't afford to run our bodies down."

As if the man had ever been sick a day in his life. He was fit and she knew that firsthand. "So *survival* is your new pickup line?"

"Do I need a pickup line?"

No. Never. But she wasn't going to admit that to him. "Where should I meet you?"

"At the ranch…in about an hour and a half?"

"Okay, I'll finish up here with Katie and meet you."

He nodded and turned to leave, then pivoted around, strode over to her and landed a kiss on her mouth that literally rocked her back on her heels. *Wow.*

He grinned, plopped his hat back on his head and then took his leave.

* * *

"Bye, Katie," Drea said, giving her friend a peck on the cheek. "I'm off now. Got a few errands to run before I head back to the ranch."

Katie shook her head. "To meet Mason. Boy, oh boy. You sure do lead an exciting life."

Drea slung her handbag over her shoulder. "We're discussing business over lunch, is all."

"Didn't sound like the two of you discussed much business last night. Don't get me wrong, I'm glad you two hooked up. It's about time."

Drea stood on the threshold of the bakery kitchen, grateful Lori was busy serving customers and no one was within earshot of their conversation. Katie had pried some deets, as she called them, out of her about last night's trip to The Baron as Drea helped bake an experimental batch of rainbow cupcakes. Katie sure knew her stuff; the cupcakes had turned out perfect. And now she was matchmaking, which wasn't allowed between close friends. Or at least it shouldn't be.

"I bet you two don't get much work done this afternoon, either. I bet he takes you somewhere really nice."

"You do have a crazy imagination."

"Just go. You don't want to leave his hunkiness waiting."

"I'm going, I'm going."

Drea left Katie in the bakery kitchen and had reached the front door when it opened suddenly and she bumped into the man walking in.

"Excuse me. Sorry," he said.

"No, no. It was my fault, too. I wasn't looking where I was…" She glanced up and found the man's eyes on her. It wasn't just any man, it was Brad. Dr. Brad Williamson, the taker of her virginity, the man who'd offered to marry her. The man she'd had to walk away from because it wouldn't be fair, since she didn't love him.

"Drea, is that you?"

She bit her lip and nodded. Too many emotions stirred inside, pain and regret being at the top. She hadn't seen Brad in ten years. But he looked the same, if a bit fuller in the face, more solid all the way around. He was in his early thirties, an age when men flourished, showing a certain mature confidence and grace. He had intelligent blue eyes, a nice tan, and his longish hair was the same sandy-blond color she remembered.

"W-what are you doing here, Brad?" she blurted. He was a blast from her past and not necessarily a welcome one. Immediately, her nerves jumped. It wasn't him, but the memory of the entire ordeal that rattled her. "I mean, I never thought I'd see you in Boone Springs."

"You and me both," he said, smiling at her as if he was really glad to see her. "But I had the opportunity to give a few interviews and lectures on my book tour not far from here, and well, when I read about the hospital fund-raiser and your part in it, I thought I'd come by and see for myself."

"You've written a book?" After college, Brad had

gone on to med school and had become a pediatrician. She knew this only because he'd texted her occasionally after the breakup, updating her, though she'd never replied. She'd just wanted that part of her life to be over. After a time, he'd stopped texting her.

"Yes, on the trials of raising a toddler."

"Do you…" She swallowed hard. "Do you have children?"

His blue eyes softened immediately and he nodded. "Two. Meggie is three, Charlie is five. Living with their mother now, but we have joint custody."

"Must be hard," Drea said.

"The kids are well-adjusted. My ex and I try our best to make sure of that. That's one reason I wrote the book. It's called *The See-Saw Effect of Parenting*."

She nodded. Brad had been destined to be a leader in his field. He was superintelligent, determined and, well, very handsome. Not that it had anything to do with anything, but she couldn't help noticing that about the man she'd singled out and seduced her first week of college, just to get back at Mason, just to prove that she was desirable. Mason's rejection that summer had her running into a stranger's arms, and lucky for her, Brad had turned out to be a decent guy. A guy who'd fallen for her, a guy who'd planned on marrying her to give their child security.

God, she'd been so confused, so scared and so damn naive.

The door chimed again and a few customers walked in and. Drea and Brad had to move over to continue the conversation. "Guess we're in the way," he said. "Do you have a few minutes…for an old friend? Just to catch up?"

She glanced at her watch. "I have a few minutes before my meeting." With Mason.

"Here?"

No, not here. Not where people might overhear their conversation. "There's a park just a few streets down. We could walk there. Did you want coffee? Or a cupcake?" she asked, figuring it was the reason he'd come.

"No, I'm good. How about you?"

She shook her head. "Katie's a friend and I've been tasting cupcakes all morning, so no. I'm definitely good."

"Well, then. Let's go." He opened the door for her and she walked out onto the busy sunny street. Donning her sunglasses, she waited for Brad. Once he caught up, after holding the door for a few more customers walking in, they headed south toward the park.

The tree-lined street looked so smalltown compared to New York, with its skyscrapers blocking the sun so that some streets were in shadow most of the time.

"How have you been?" he asked, keeping stride with her.

"I've been really good. This project is very special to me, since it'll fund a cardiac wing at the hospital in my hometown. I'm here for a few more weeks."

"Are you okay with me looking you up?"

"Sure. It's…good to see you, Brad."

"Same here. I, uh, think about you and what you've taken on here. Because of your mom?"

She stopped and stared into his blue eyes. "You remember?"

"Of course I remember, Drea. When we met, your mother's death and your helplessness over it were a big part of who you were. And now you're doing something to make a difference. I remember you'd always wanted that."

She looked away for a second, tears misting her eyes. She was touched that he remembered what made her tick, how vulnerable she'd been when they'd met. "You're right. It was."

When he smiled at her, her spirits lifted a bit. She hadn't been thrilled to bump into him, but now, after talking with him a few minutes, she began to relax.

When they reached the park, they took a seat on a bench facing the playground. A few toddlers were giving their moms a merry chase around the slide.

"How about you?" he asked. "Did you ever marry? Do you have a family?"

"No and no. I'm married to my job right now."

"I hear that." He didn't criticize her for not settling down, like so many others had. If a woman closing in on thirty wasn't married, well then, either there was something wrong with her or she was too ambitious for her own good.

They spent the next hour catching up on news, keeping the conversation light without mentioning the heartache they'd both endured. Brad seemed to hold no grudge toward her. Even though he'd been in love with her and would've married her, baby or not, she'd broken up with him after she'd miscarried. She'd made one mistake after another, but marrying Brad when she didn't love him would've been cruel.

Drea had learned a valuable lesson. Love is only right when it's two-sided and equal. There could be no imbalance.

Brad told her about himself, his years in med school and how he'd opened a pediatric practice in Manhattan and gotten married shortly after that. When she asked about his children, his face lit up and he spent a good deal of time on his little Meg and Charlie.

"I'll be in town until your fund-raiser," he said. "I plan on making a donation."

She smiled. "That's wonderful. We have lofty goals, so it will really be appreciated."

"Drea, do you mind if I ask you a personal question?"

Her heart stopped. *Oh no. Here it comes.* She braced herself. "What would you like to know?"

"Are you seeing anyone right now?"

That was totally unexpected. She fidgeted with her blouse, her head down. So he wasn't going to dredge up the past, or excoriate her for breaking his heart. "No, not really." It wasn't as if she was dating Mason or anything. *Just sleeping with him.*

Brad's face broke out in a big smile. It was almost laughable how obvious he was. "Well then, I'd like to ask you to dinner one night."

Why? She wanted to know, but she held her tongue.

"As a friend," he added. "I'm staying close by and have the book signing in a few days, but I'd love to catch up more over a nice relaxing dinner."

She hadn't expected a dinner invitation. Sure, she could tell him she was too busy, but he was looking at her earnestly and what would it hurt? Maybe it would actually be therapeutic to spend time with him. How odd, but just being with him this past hour had helped relieve some of the remorse she felt over the whole situation.

"I think, maybe…" She tilted her head. "Yes."

"Great, I'll give you a call. Are you at the same number?"

"Let me give you my new one."

After they traded phone numbers, she stood up and he rose, too, though a bit reluctantly. "I really should get on with my errands," she said, excusing herself.

"Okay. Thanks for today," he replied, taking her hand in what was definitely not a shake but a touch of reconnection. "I should be going, too."

And that's when she realized…

Holy crap! She was late for her meeting with Mason.

Mason glanced at his watch for the third time as he paced up and down along the wraparound veranda at his house. He got out his phone, debating whether to text Drea. She was late, but only by fifteen minutes, and though he was anxious to see her again, to spend time with her, he didn't want to come off as… what? Pushy? Needy? Worried?

Because he was worried about her. She wasn't one

to be late. She was usually professional and prompt. He didn't know where it was coming from, but it gave him hives thinking something might've happened to her.

Risk stepped onto the porch, a beer in his hand. He lifted the bottle to his lips and took a swig before turning to Mason. "You're pacing? Bro, that's not like you. You must be waiting on someone." His brother had a penchant for stating the obvious.

Mason gave him a look.

Risk grinned. "You're waiting on Drea. Well, isn't that something."

"We have an appointment, about work."

"Right..." Risk smirked before taking another swig. "I wouldn't worry overly much, Mase. She's fine. When I was in town, I drove right past her. She was sitting on a park bench with some guy. The two looked pretty cozy, if you ask me. She probably lost track of time is all."

Mason eyed him. "Some guy? Who was he?"

"I have no idea. Never saw the man before. But he was all buttoned up in a suit and tie, and looked like he wasn't from around here. Just my observation."

Mason cleared his throat. "Okay, thanks."

Just then Mason's phone buzzed. It was an incoming text from Drea.

Sorry, my errands ran long. I'll be there soon.

Mason stared at the message a few seconds, relieved and curious.

"That her?" Risk asked.

"Yeah, she's running late."

Risk put a hand on his shoulder. "You care about her? And give me the truth, because lying to your brother is punishable by a swift kick in the ass."

"Like to see you try." It was an old joke between them. Risk had always stood his ground, no matter that Mason was older and stronger. But that was Risk, always snarky, always trying to defy the odds. He was the last one to give relationship advice. He went through women like a cat licking up bowls of sweet milk: quick and none too pretty.

"I'm serious," he said.

"Of course I care about Drea. She's Drew's daughter and I've known her most of my life. That's all there is to it."

"Okay, bro. Just thinking it would be pretty cool if you did. You've sorta been *not living* these past two years, you know what I mean?"

He knew. He just didn't like the idea that his whole family was worried about him. They didn't understand how grief had to work its way out of you, and there was no speeding the process. "Yeah, I do know."

And now, just the thought of Drea on her way to meet him sent a jolt of adrenaline speeding through his system. She'd been the only woman to break through the wall of his grief, and he would welcome that relief for the time she had left in Texas.

Thirty minutes later, Drea pulled up to the house and dashed up the steps. He was waiting on the porch for her, reading local news on his phone. It had been hard to focus, and as soon as he laid eyes on her, his body jerked to attention as if Drea had defibrillated him with paddles to his chest.

"So sorry I'm late," she said, her face flushed.

"It's okay. What happened?"

"I lost track of time running errands. I have a lot on my mind these days. I hope I didn't mess up your schedule for the day."

So she wasn't going to tell him about the guy. It was probably nothing, maybe a meeting with someone related to the project. And little did she know he'd cleared his schedule this afternoon to be with her. "Not at all. But I am hungry. How about you?"

"Yes."

"Okay, let's get going."

"Where?"

"You'll see."

Mason led her to his truck, opened the door for her and watched as she slid onto the seat. Her dress hiked up her thighs, giving him a clear view of her long tanned legs. Legs that had driven him insane wrapped around him last night.

When he was with Drea the world seemed right, but he was taking this one day at a time and living in the moment. Because it would end. It had to end. He was counting on it ending. That was the only way he could justify this brief interlude with her. He wasn't ready for anything permanent, anything that could go awry and scar him deeply. He hadn't healed from his first heartache. He didn't need another. Drea was leaving soon, and they would part ways. But for now, he wanted to spend as much time with her as he could.

A few minutes later, he parked the truck and helped Drea climb out. Holding her in his arms, he bent his head and kissed her lightly.

Her eyelids fluttered and he wanted more, but he held back, straining his willpower. "Close your eyes and come with me."

"What?"

He put his fingertip to her nose. "Just do it."

She closed her eyes, a big smile on her face. "I don't like surprises, just so you know."

"Trust me, you'll like this one."

He took her hand and guided her down a grassy pathway that led to the spot he'd picked out just for her. "Okay, open your eyes."

The sound of ducks quacking reached Drea's ears first, and then came a noisy flutter of wings. But when she popped her eyes open, the first thing she spotted was a café table dressed with a white table-cloth and two chairs set up on the bank of a small, secluded lake she'd never been to. A cut-crystal vase filled with pearl-white roses served as the centerpiece and wine was chilling in a bucket. The whole scene looked too good to be true.

A family of ducks glided across the water just at the right moment, as if it their swim was choreographed. She smiled at the sight they made. "Wow. What's going on?" She hadn't expected anything like this.

"Lunch."

"I know, silly." She turned to Mason, noting a gleam of satisfaction in his eyes. "But why?"

He shrugged, a myriad of emotions flowing through his expression. She didn't know if she'd get the truth out of him by the look on his face.

"You've been working hard. I thought you'd like a quiet lunch out here where it's open and peaceful."

"You went to a lot of trouble," she said, truly touched. Her heart warmed every time Mason did something nice for her like this. And to think she'd nearly canceled lunch with him today. But she knew she was treading dangerous ground. "Thank you."

He smiled. "You're welcome."

"Are we still on Boone land?" she asked, although she was pretty sure of the answer.

"Yep. This is Hidden Lake. I named it myself."

"You did? When?"

"Just now." He laughed and so did she. "Seems appropriate, doesn't it?"

"You have a knack," she said. "But I never knew this lake existed."

"It's been here the entire time, but through years of drought it had nearly dried up, the water level too low for it to be considered anything but a big puddle. We've had some good rainfall the past few years. And now Hidden Lake is once more."

"It's beautiful."

"Yeah, it's a nice spot." He held out a chair for her. "Ready?"

"I am." She took a seat and Mason served her one

dish after another. The food was catered by Bountiful, the best restaurant in town.

She feasted on lemon chicken, shrimp risotto and roasted vegetables. There were three kinds of bread and a nice bottle of white wine. She nibbled on her meal, enjoying the ambience, but the best thing of all about the scenery was the tall, handsome man in front of her.

Mason's gaze never strayed from hers. He chewed his food and looked at her. He sipped his wine and watched her sip hers. The conversation was light and fun, and he smiled a lot, which made her smile a lot, too.

Peace surrounded her and she squeezed her eyes closed, soaking it all in. It was truly what she'd needed today. "Thank you," she said. "I almost don't want to spoil this by talking about work."

"Work?" he asked.

"You said you needed advice. What was that all about?"

"I do need advice, but it's not about work."

She chewed on her lower lip a moment. "Then what is it about?"

"The beach house in Los Angeles. Missy has a potential buyer for it, but she wanted to give me the first option to purchase. I really don't know what I want to do."

"And you think I can help with your decision?"

He nodded. But she wasn't sure she wanted to be included in such a major decision in his life.

"You've seen it. What do you think?" he asked.

"I love it. I mean, what's not to love? But it's not up to me. Would you actually use it as a second home? It's definitely a big change from Boone Springs. Do you think you'd be comfortable there?"

Mason shrugged. "I was, when I was with you."

Oh... Her heart did a little flip at his unguarded reply. She'd had a great time while she'd been there, too, but she couldn't make a big deal about it. Mason was talking past history. He had to think about the future, and that didn't include her. "That was a one-time thing," she said softly.

Mason stared at her for several seconds and nodded slowly, conceding the point. "Yeah."

Then he rose from his seat. "Take a walk with me along the lake."

"That sounds nice," she said, rising in turn.

He took her hand and led her down to the lake's grassy edge. He pointed at the cute duck family still swimming nearby, and they laughed together as Mason took her into his arms. Her heart nearly stopped when he kissed her fully, thoroughly, as only he could do. "Meet me tonight, Drea. Be with me."

Drea murmured her agreement.

Because she just couldn't help herself.

Eight

Drea didn't know where the time had gone. There were only six days left before the big event. In the days since their lunch by Hidden Lake, she'd mostly been holed up with Mason, working. But when they weren't working, they were playing. Mason had re-taught her the art of horseback riding and they'd gone riding several times on Rising Springs land. It *was* just like riding a bike. She'd never really forgotten. Once the reins were in her hands, it had all clicked again. She was thankful to him for making her take that first ride, and for the long walks, the meals they shared and especially for their secret nights at The Baron.

Tonight, she had dinner plans with her father. It would be just the two of them. As she walked up the steps of the cottage, she realized how full her life was right now. Family, friends and the attention of her fantasy man all put a smile on her face.

She no longer counted the days before she would return to New York and resume her life there. She was falling in love with Boone Springs again, something she thought would never happen. She questioned it every day, tried to find fault in her thought patterns, but that was just it. It wasn't so much what she was thinking, but more what she was feeling. And those emotions were getting stronger every day.

"Daddy, I'm home." She entered the house and found her father at the kitchen table, going through a big wooden box she'd never seen before.

"Hi, dear girl." He quickly closed the box and latched it.

"What do you have there?" she asked, more than mildly curious now that he'd seemed so secretive about it.

"Just some things from the past."

"Mom's things?"

He nodded and shrugged. "Yeah, there's some of your mama's stuff in here."

"Can I see?"

She sat down next to him, watching him carefully. Fear entered his eyes, followed by a look of resignation. Or was she mistaken? Maybe the box just held mementos. When her mother died, her father had given her keepsakes of her mom that she would always treasure, including a birthstone ring, her wedding ring, a favorite silver locket and a pair of diamond earrings.

"It's just some old stuff. I haven't gone through this box in a long time."

"Why now?"

"Maybe because you're here visiting." Her father opened it and revealed a treasure trove of clippings and old ticket stubs to concerts, movies and dances. "I saved all this. I don't know why."

"I do, Dad. It's a testament to your life with Mom. It's like your history together." She picked up a photo she'd never seen before, of a very young couple standing in front of a diner, obviously crazy about each other. "When's this from?"

"Oh, sweet girl. That's one of our first dates. I took your mama to some fancy restaurant and she took one look at the prices and said she'd rather have burgers and fries. Back then, I was working for my daddy and he was harder on me than on his crew. Said I had to work my way up the ladder if I wanted a piece of Thundering Hills one day, so money was tight and your mama, even then, had my back. She wasn't going to have me break the bank to impress her. I think I fell in love with her that night, Drea. She was something."

Tears welled in Drea's eyes. But she wasn't sad, not at all. She was truly amazed at the beautiful love the two of them had for each other. Clearly, her father had adored his Maria.

Drew shared several more memories with her and showed her a couple trinkets that made her smile. And then he brought out an unsealed envelope. He tapped it against his other hand a few times and turned to her. "Tell me, Drea," he said, his gravelly voice sharper than usual. "You and Mason are getting close, right? I see the way he looks at you."

What? Goodness, she wasn't prepared for a question like that. "Dad, we're working on the fund-raiser together. We both have a vested interest. And no, I could never get seriously involved with a Boone. You know why. I can never forgive them for what they did to our family."

"Drea, my brain hasn't gone to seed yet. I know you're going out at night. I'm assuming you're meeting with Mason. You're a grown woman and it's none of my business, but I got a reason to be asking."

She felt heat rising to her face; she was probably turning the shade of a ripe tomato. "Dad, you know?"

"I do now," he said without sarcasm.

"It's… Mason and I…we're just casual."

Her father's bushy brows rose. "Doesn't matter. I've been talking to Lottie and she thinks I've been doing you an injustice. Maybe I have. Maybe I was just making myself look better in your eyes by putting the blame on the Boones all these years. I'm sorry, Drea."

"For what, Dad? What are you talking about?" Her heart began to pound as dread overtook her. She'd never heard such remorse in her father's tone.

"All those years ago, after your mama died, I let the ranch go to ruin. I couldn't deal with the loss, the pressure and raising you. I was a terrible father,

Drea. I know that, and I'm making amends now, by telling you the truth. I didn't go to the Boones for a loan like I told you. They didn't deny me. The fact is, I didn't ask them to help me save my ranch. I practically begged them to take it off my hands. I knew they'd give me a fair price. I made the deal with them, specifically stipulating that the money would go into a fund for your college education. I didn't trust myself with the money. I knew I'd drink it away. That's at least one good thing I did. I wanted to protect you, from myself."

Bile rose in her throat and she felt dizzy. "Dad... are you saying that they didn't steal Thundering Hills out from under you? Are you saying the Boones paid for my education?"

He ran a hand down his face. "Yeah, darlin' girl. That's the truth. It's all here in this personal agreement I made with Henry Boone."

Drea snatched the envelope out of his hands, opened it and took out the written agreement. She scanned the contents quickly, her eyes keying in on words that verified her father's claims until there was no doubt. "Oh my God. Why? Why didn't you just tell me the truth?"

"And admit yet another failure to my only daughter? I was a coward. It was easier to let the Boones take the blame. To let you think they'd robbed you of your birthright, when actually, I was guilty of that myself. It's eaten at me all these years. And now, Drea, I see you and Mason together, and if there's a chance for the two of you, well, I couldn't let that get in the way of your happiness. I couldn't bear it, not again. Lottie said it's about time."

"Lottie?" It was the second time he'd mentioned her. "So everyone knew the truth but me?"

Her father shook his head. "Not everyone. We kept the terms of the agreement private. Let people come to their own conclusions. But the Boone brothers know, yes."

"And you let me berate them, hate them, think the very worst of the people who actually saved your hide?"

"I'm sorry, Drea. Truly sorry."

"Sorry's not enough, Dad. Not nearly…enough."

Limbs shaking, tears spilling down her cheeks, she dashed out of the room. When she got to her bedroom, she slammed the door and then slumped against it, slowly sinking into a heap on the floor. She'd been betrayed and lied to one too many times. Everything she thought she knew about her life had just been whisked away. Was she overreacting? Maybe, but why did she always have to be the grownup? Why couldn't she be the kid, the one who needed tending, the one who needed comfort? She wanted to fall apart. She needed to. It was her right, something she'd been deprived of for too many years. She didn't care if this episode would send her father back to the bottle. She'd lived with that fear for too long.

This was her time to grieve and she wasn't holding back.

"Drea, please. I'm sorry," her father said from the other side of the door.

"Go away, Dad. Leave me alone."

It was a while before she heard him sigh heavily and walk away, his footfalls receding until there was no sound.

No sound but the deep, stabbing sobs racking her body.

It was after eleven when Mason got the text from Drea.

I need to see you tonight. Can we meet?

Mason was at home at Rising Springs, already in bed, going over the final details of the fund-raiser. It was hard to believe the event was coming up so quickly and he'd wanted to make sure he had everything covered. He didn't like leaving things to chance. That's what he and Drea had in common: they paid attention to details. She was having dinner with her dad tonight and they hadn't planned on seeing each other, so getting this text message from her this late surprised him.

What's going on? he typed.

Please, I need to see you.

At The Baron?

Yes, in thirty minutes?

I'll be there.

Mason wasn't going to pass up an opportunity to see Drea. The nights when they weren't together felt strange to him and he didn't much like analyzing why that was, especially after the conversation he'd had with Larissa's mother earlier in the day. She'd let him know she and Larissa's father were driving to town, coming all the way from Arizona, and they wanted to see him. He knew why. They were coming to lay flowers on Larissa's grave on the second anniversary of her death. Two years had gone by. Two. In one respect, the time had seemed to crawl by as he relived his wife's final days and the singeing loss he felt even before she'd taken her last breaths. But it also seemed as if the past two years had flown by. How could it be both? And how could he have lived two full years without Larissa by his side?

Now, as he headed to the hotel to meet Drea, he was conflicted and guilt-ridden. His in-laws were coming to town. They were coming to help him grieve, to honor their daughter's memory, to feel closer to her. But all he could think about was Drea.

Yet her ominous text message made him nervous. She'd never been cryptic before. She'd never initiated their meeting. So he pressed his foot down on the gas pedal and sped through the relatively empty roads leading to town. He made it in quick time and entered his suite before Drea got there.

He was just removing his jacket when he heard her knock.

He opened the door and she flew into his arms. He stood there stunned for a second, until her warm breath caressed his face and she planted a kiss on him that had him forgetting his first name. Hell, she didn't come up for air, just kept kissing him, tearing at the buttons of his shirt, splaying her soft palms on his skin, making him sizzle, making him want.

He slammed the door shut behind her. He didn't know where the hell this was coming from, but he wasn't about to question it. Or her. His body reacted, as it always did from Drea's touch, and he was immediately caught up in the urgency, the intensity. He tore away at her clothes, too, pulling her blouse out of her jeans, unbuttoning it between kisses. She removed her bra without his help and her beautiful breasts sprang free.

He was hard and ready. This aggressive, wild Drea was a big, big turn-on.

He held her long hair away from her chest and bent his head, moistening one rosy areola with his mouth, his tongue, causing the tip to perk up. She was gorgeous, too damn beautiful for his sanity. She whimpered, a cry of need that pierced his soul. She was on fire, hot and frenzied, and he wasn't far behind. He removed the rest of her clothes, then his. But when he stopped kissing her to lead her into the bedroom, she shook her head and kept him right there, as if even the slightest separation would be too much for her.

After pressing her against the door, he had just enough time to grab a condom and sheath himself before lifting her back into his arms. Instinctively, she wrapped her legs around his waist and her kisses became softer, slower, as if she were savoring him, as if she were committing this to memory. Her soft mewling nearly killed him. He was too far gone to play games. His need to join their bodies was intense, ferocious. He picked up the pace, taking charge now, kissing her thoroughly, nipping at her swollen lips, tasting her hot skin and trailing a path down her throat.

He positioned her over him, his hands cupping her butt, and then guided her down onto his shaft. She was warm and wet and the look of pure pleasure on her face was so damn perfect.

It was fast, fiery, frenzied and about the most incredible thing he'd ever done with a woman. When she cried out, her throaty sounds of pure bliss sent him over the edge.

He tightened his hold on her, feverishly moving, his body desperately seeking the ultimate prize. Then, making one deep, long, final thrust with his hips, he let out a groan of contentment that shattered him.

He was done.

Totally destroyed.

He held on to Drea and carried her to the bedroom.

That was when he got a good look at her face. Her pretty green eyes were rimmed with red.

She'd been crying.

Mason lay with Drea nestled in his arms, her head resting on his shoulder. He stroked her arm, absorbing the softness of her skin. She was quiet now, seemingly drained of energy. Why had she been crying? He had no clue. She'd come here like a woman on a mission, and it was only afterward that he took note of her distress. "Are you okay?" he asked quietly.

"No," she replied. "I'm not okay. I haven't been okay for a long time, Mason."

The sadness in her voice nearly broke him. "Why?"

She sighed deeply, her voice brittle. "I found out the truth about Thundering Hills tonight. My father told me…everything." She nibbled on her lip a moment and then continued. "At first I didn't believe it. My entire life I was led to believe one thing, only to learn that none of it was true."

She lifted her head from his chest and those sad, sad eyes touched something deep inside him. "I've misjudged you, Mason. I've been awful to you."

He rubbed her shoulder and smiled. "What are you talking about, sweetheart?"

"I hated and resented you for years."

"I know."

"Why didn't you tell me the truth? Why did you let me go on hating you? Why did you lie to me all those times? It wasn't fair, Mason. It wasn't fair to let me go on believing the worst about your family."

"It was the way your father wanted it. He made a pact with my dad to keep the terms of their agreement a secret. He must've had his reasons for keeping you in the dark. And as far as we're concerned, I always thought you'd figure out on your own that you didn't hate me."

She frowned. "Because you're so darn irresistible?"

"Because you're a smart woman and eventually you would see me for the man I really am."

"To think I've blamed your entire family, I've had terrible thoughts of them all this time. I thought you were all greedy and now I find that it wasn't anything but kindness and generosity. The Boones are responsible for me getting my college degree, for heaven's sake."

"Your father did right by you, Drea. At least in that way, he put your needs above his own."

"He didn't want me to see him as a complete failure. He told me so tonight, how he put the blame for our loss on the Boones. It wasn't right or fair of him and I let him know it. I was really hard on him tonight."

"Is that why you're so upset?"

"Yes, it's a lot to take in." She ran her hand down her face, then gently tapped her cheek. "Do I look terrible?"

"You look beautiful, Drea."

He sat up on the bed, drawing her with him, and wrapped his arms around her. "Did he say why he chose tonight to tell you?"

"It was your aunt Lottie. She told him it was time for me to know the truth. Gosh, I wish one of you would've told me before now. I'm feeling betrayed… by everyone. But I also think the two of them were conspiring about…"

"About?"

"About us… They think—no, my father knows I've

been seeing you. He said he didn't want my feelings about the Boones to stand in our way."

"Our way?" Mason wasn't sure what she was getting at. She was leaving after this weekend. She had a life to go back to.

"I think he meant just in case we fall for each other," she said, so softly he could barely hear her.

Mason bit down, keeping his mouth clamped shut. Drea had to know going in he wasn't available. Not emotionally. Not in any way. Just the thought of a permanent relationship made him shudder. He wasn't ready for anything like that. He didn't know if he ever would be. The thought of loving someone again, and losing her, scared the hell out of him. Yes, if it was going to be any woman, he'd want it to be Drea. But he just couldn't…go there again. Call him a coward, but his head and his gut told him no, no, no.

"I mean," she said quietly, "we aren't falling for each other, are we?"

There was such hope in her voice, such tenderness, as if the answer could break her.

He shifted away from her on the bed. Here they were, stark naked after a blistering night of wild sex. He felt closer to Drea than any woman he'd met in the past two years. He liked her, admired her and cared deeply for her. Yet he didn't have an answer for her. He didn't know what to say. She'd already been hurt enough.

All he could do was speak the truth. He stared into the distance, keeping his back to her. "You're leaving in a few days, Drea."

He hoped like hell the words came off gentle, kind. It was a statement of fact. Not a yes, not a no. Well, maybe a no. He'd made it clear he wasn't committing to anything.

He turned to her finally and stared into her eyes, hoping to see understanding, a note of agreement. But all he saw was her attempt to mask pain.

It hurt like hell seeing the emotions pass over her face, one after another, as she tried to conceal what she was really feeling. At this moment, she didn't have to hate him; he was doing a pretty good job of hating himself.

"Right," she said quietly. "I… This has been great. But it's…nothing."

The *nothing* stung. She hadn't meant it to, she'd merely been searching for words, and he hated that he'd put her in that position.

She rose then and headed for the living room, where she'd left her clothes. "I'd better get home. It's very late and we have a big day tomorrow. Sean and the band are coming."

"Drea?" Mason got up and followed her. "Let me drive you home."

"Really, Mason. I have to go. Just know I don't h-hate you anymore."

With her clothes thrown on haphazardly, she picked up her bag, slung it over her shoulder and took her leave.

Last night, after learning the truth, Drea had finally been free to open her heart and let her emotions fly. Now what she felt for Mason was love. She *loved* him. She loved him so much the burn of his rejection seared her heart. After the last time he'd rejected her, she should've learned her lesson. She should have known it would never work out between the two of them. She'd been a fool, a silly fool for falling in love with a man who was still painfully in love with his dead wife.

He wasn't a bad man. He wasn't horrible. He was loyal and true blue. For some reason, she'd been the woman to wake his sexual senses after two years of hibernation. She'd made him come alive and sparked something in him he thought long dead. She would always have that. She'd gotten over Mason once before, and would just have to find a way to do it again.

While her heart bled for a love that would go nowhere, she had to forge on. She had a job to do and that meant dealing with Mason. Her wounds were raw and open, but this project was too important to her. She couldn't fall apart. She had to maintain, to keep up, appearances.

Drea poured tea into her mother's favorite hand-painted floral teapot and walked into the dining room to rejoin Lottie. She'd invited the older woman over after Drew left to visit a friend earlier this morning.

Drea's relationship with her father was still on rocky ground. She hadn't had a chance to speak to him yet, to clear the air and perhaps try to forgive him. She'd put that on the very long list of things she needed to do.

"Lottie, would you care for more tea?"

"Sure, thank you. It's delicious. I'm so glad you invited me over. We don't see enough of each other."

"I know. I'm sorry. I've been superbusy."

"Mason tells me you've been doing a fantastic job."

At the mention of Mason's name, she frowned. It was automatic, and she righted herself, but she didn't fool Lottie. Her eyes softened and she gave Drea a knowing look. "Something tells me this is more than a social visit. You need to talk to me, don't you, sweetheart?"

Drea nodded, sinking down in the chair. Tears welled in her eyes. "I do."

"Is it your dad or Mason?"

She smiled halfheartedly. "Both."

"What is it?"

"I need some direction, Lottie, and I need to tell someone the whole truth. I thought I could tell Mason last night when we were together. Instead we ended up…well, breaking up. Which is so dumb because you actually have to be a couple in order to break up. But we never were, not really."

"Oh, sweetheart…you love him."

She nodded. "I do. But he isn't over Larissa, and maybe he never will be."

Drea spent the next half hour pouring her heart out. She explained how she knew the truth about Thundering Hills now, and the Boones' part in all of it. She told Lottie how she'd fought with her father, unable to see the logic in what he'd done, the lies he'd told.

She told Lottie everything, from her infatuation

with Mason and his abrupt rejection years ago to how she'd run into the arms of Brad Williamson, conceived a child with him and miscarried. Her scars were finally exposed, and it was brutal revealing all the secrets she'd held inside. All the pain and injury she'd suffered through the years.

Lottie held her hand through most of it, and wiped Drea's cheeks when tears flooded her face. "I've loved Mason, hated him, and now I'm so terribly out of my element I don't know what to do. Brad is a doctor now and he's here in Boone Springs for a short time. I've spoken to him. He's a really good guy. I hate that I hurt him. He was ready to marry me, and that would've been a big mistake. I didn't love him. So how can I fault Mason for not loving me, and easing out of our relationship, when I did the same thing to Brad?"

"You know what I think?" Lottie said. "My nephew has been living in the past for far too long. He's got to get over it."

Drea sucked in a sob to steady her breath. "No one can make him do that, Lottie."

"Don't be so sure about that." Lottie's voice took on a mischievous tone. "Will you be joining us for dinner tonight, sweetheart?"

"I have to be there," she said. She wouldn't let her queasy stomach stop her from doing her job. The Boones were hosting a dinner for The Band Blue. "It's the band's first night in town."

"Good."

Drea dabbed at her face with a napkin. She was too busy for any more crying jags. And shedding her burden to Lottie had been the best therapy. At least now someone knew the entire truth. At least Drea had someone to confide in.

Lottie finished her tea and rose. "Don't you worry about a thing."

Drea wished she had her confidence. Her life was a total mess. And perhaps most of it was her own fault. That's what stung the worst.

When Lottie put out her arms, Drea got up and flowed into them. Lottie was warm and soft and welcoming, all the things Drea's life had been missing. She closed her eyes and absorbed the comfort, missing her mother so very much, but grateful for this woman who had loved them both.

They hugged a good long time, and then Lottie spoke softly. "You're an amazing woman, Drea. I love you with all of my heart."

It was the best thing she could've said to her. "I love you too, Lottie."

Lottie pulled away and looked into Drea's eyes. "Thanks for the tea, sweetheart. I'll see you tonight."

"Yes, I'll be there." Suddenly Drea felt stronger, a bit more like herself. She had a job to do, and she'd focus on that for the next three days.

As Lottie exited the cottage, she heard noises coming from the back woodshed. In the past, when Drew had been up to it, he'd built things there. Of course, those days had been few and far between. Now, letting her curiosity get the better of her, Lottie went behind the house to investigate.

She found Drew at a worktable, his jacket slung over an old chair. He must've just been dropped off by his friend. She thought it odd that he hadn't come right into the cottage.

Then she saw him lift a bottle of Jack Daniels from the table, the amber liquid swishing around inside. She had only a moment to react. Only a moment to stop the foolish man from doing something he'd regret later on. "Drew, don't you dare take a swig of that bottle."

He jumped and turned around quickly, still clutching the bottle in his hand. "Geesh, woman. You nearly scared me half to death. What are you—" Then he blinked and his eyes darkened as her words finally sank in. He looked from her to the bottle. Then back at her again.

His shoulders slumped and his eyes hardened. "Why in hell would I take a swig of shellac, Lottie Sue Brown?"

Lottie took a better look at the bottle. It said Jack Daniels on the label, but there was a thin strip of masking tape around the center spelling out SHEL-LAC. "I, uh, it's just that I know you and Drea had some issues to deal with and I, uh…couldn't see too well with the morning shadows and all."

"You think a spat with my daughter would've turned me to drink again?" His voice was quiet. "You have no faith in me, Lottie. None at all, and that's not about to change, is it? Don't answer. I won't believe anything you say right now. You want to know what I'm doing with this bottle, which I borrowed, by the way, from my friend Rusty? I'm trying to shine up Drea's softball trophies to give to her. I never made it to many of the games back then, and these things mean a lot to me now. I'm always looking for ways to make amends with my daughter."

Lottie had stepped in it now. She'd been quite effectively told off. Oh boy, she'd let preconceived notions about Drew influence her judgment. If only she'd kept her trap shut. If only she'd had more faith in him. He'd been trying to prove to her he was a changed man, but now she feared she'd destroyed any trust they had between them. "Oh, Drew. Forgive me. I'm sorry, very sorry."

He turned away from her. "Lottie, just let me get back to this."

"But Drew—"

"Go, Lottie. You've said enough this morning."

And suddenly, her heart ached and her stomach burned.

Had one incident of mistrust ruined things with him forever?

Nine

Drea straightened her snow-white, curve-hugging dress and knocked on the front door of the Boone mansion. She was flying solo tonight, her father opting to stay home. They'd had a good long talk this afternoon and had agreed to put the past behind them. She could forgive him for past mistakes, but it would be a long time before she would truly be over it. She loved her dad and he loved her. All they could do was go from there.

She wore red high heel pumps and the silver jewelry she loved so much. The Boones' housekeeper, Jessica, opened the door and greeted her. It appeared the entire staff was on call tonight. Drea had no idea of the scope of the dinner, but apparently the Boones had invited more than family. The sheriff of Boone

County and several hospital administrators were in attendance, as well as the mayor. Mason's cousins, Rafe, Nash and Cord, were also in attendance. They were part-time cattle ranchers, among other things, and obviously big country and western fans. So of course they were invited to meet the band.

"Drea, you look drop-dead gorgeous," Risk said, being the first to grab her hand and lead her into the fray. The house was hopping with laughter and music.

"Thank you. Are Sean and the band here yet?"

"Yep, they're out back. Come with me." Risk kept a tight hold of her hand as he led her to the poolside area. It was quieter out here and cooler.

"Wow, this is quite a welcome for the band."

She shivered a bit and Risk took note. "You need a drink to warm you up."

"I won't refuse. Just one."

They wandered over to a bar set up under a pillared deck. "What'll it be?"

"White wine, please."

Risk shook his head. "Make that two whiskey sours," he told the bartender.

"Risk!" She laughed, finally able to let loose with the Boones, finally able to see them for the good men they were. "Why'd you bother to ask me?"

He shrugged. "White wine won't warm you up, sweetheart. Take it from me. You need something stronger."

"I do, do I? And why is that?"

He was charming and quite a player.

"Baby, that dress you're wearing exposes more

skin than it covers. Don't get me wrong, I'm digging it, and I would offer to keep you snuggled tight tonight, but I think my brother would have me hung from the highest rafter."

She tilted her head and stared at him. Risk handed her the drink, and took his own as he pointed toward Mason, who was standing alone by the side of the house, watching her. She shivered again and glanced away. She couldn't give in to Mason's penetrating stares. He'd made up his mind and that was that.

"What's going on between you two?" Risk asked.

"As of tonight, not a thing," she answered, drinking deep from her glass.

"Well, in that case," he said, bending his head and kissing her cheek, "do I get a chance at keeping you warm tonight?"

She smiled at him. "I think the drink you fixed me up with is doing the job."

"Damn. Should've gotten you the white wine, after all," he replied, and both of them laughed.

After finishing her drink, she walked over to a group conversing with the band. Sean spotted her and broke away from the others. "Hey, Drea. Good to see you."

"Sean, it's good to see you, too."

He hugged her, a shy kind of hug that tickled her to death. She gave him a hug back.

"This is great. The Boones sure know how to do it up, don't they?"

"Yes, they sure do. I take it you got in okay today? All set up in your hotel?"

"Yep, the hotel is really cool. Alan has no complaints and we're all happy to be doing this gig."

"I'm happy, too. Listen, about the Dream Date event, we have it all set. Do you have any questions or concerns? I hope you'll let me know, since I was the one who kinda got you involved with it."

"Nope. I have no concerns."

"That's fantastic."

Mason approached, eyeing her before greeting Sean. It was *Business with Mason* all over again. It didn't matter that he looked fine, in a form-fitting charcoal suit with no tie, or that his hair was just as she liked it, brushed back with the very tips curling up at the collar. She could do this. She could. She entered into the conversation, smiling, and enjoyed getting to know Sean a little better.

A few minutes later, Sean was pulled away and she was left standing with Mason. "I think everything is ready for the big day," she said brightly. "I'm confident that, as long as the weather holds, we'll be able to pull it off."

Mason eyes were dark and serious, and when he opened his mouth to speak she shook her head immediately. If it wasn't going to be work talk, she wanted no part of it. "Don't, Mason. There's nothing more to say."

Lottie approached then, looking dazzling in a blue floral chiffon dress, on the arm of…Brad Williamson. Drea was too stunned to utter a word. Brad was smiling at her, looking a little sheepish, as well.

"Hello, you two," Lottie said. "Mason, I'd like you to meet Dr. Brad Williamson. Brad's visiting here from the East Coast. He's a dear friend of Drea's and so I thought it fitting that he join us tonight. They've known each other since college, right, Drea?"

She nodded. "Yes, that's right." Wasn't it just a few hours ago she'd been pouring out her heart to Lottie about Brad, Mason, her father? Goodness, Lottie didn't let up.

While the two men shook hands, Lottie's eyes met hers.

"Nice to meet you," Brad said to Mason. "Drea's told me all about the fund-raiser. I'm on board. It's an important thing you're doing."

"Thank you. We think so, too," Mason said. Then he clamped his mouth shut, glancing at her with a question in his eyes.

"Lottie, may I have a word with you?" Drea didn't know what exactly Lottie had hoped would happen by inviting Brad to the dinner party.

"Oh, uh, I can't right now. Chef needs me in the kitchen. You three have a nice talk and I'll see you all later."

An awkward moment passed. Mason remained tight-lipped.

"Brad, how did you meet Lottie?" Drea asked. It was the question of the day.

Brad looked handsome tonight, dressed in a casual gray suit. His eyes were mesmerizing, almost a transparent blue. "Well, we met at the local bookstore. I was signing copies of my book and we got to talking about the fund-raiser. So when she found out I was a country fan and that I knew you, she invited me. I'm sorry I didn't run it by you first. You're okay with this, aren't you? Since we never did get to have dinner together, I was hoping—"

"It's perfectly fine, Brad. I'm glad you're here."

"Then I'm glad I am, too." He smiled. "You look… *amazing.*"

She didn't dare glance at Mason, but she sensed him stiffening up. "Thank you."

Drea's nerves were shot. She was standing between the two men who'd had a major impact in her life and she had no idea what was going on in either of their minds.

Lucky for her, one of the hospital administrators joined the conversation and she was able to slip away leaving the men behind. She walked out the front door and kept on walking. She was on the path to her father's house, her mind all mixed up. She wasn't sure where she belonged. Or whom she belonged with. It was dark and the path she traveled was lit only by moonlight, so when she heard footsteps behind her, she sucked in a breath and turned around. "What are you doing here?" she asked, seeing it was Mason.

"Walking you home," he said casually, as if he hadn't just broken her heart last night. As if he had a right to walk her anywhere.

"Not necessary. I'm capable of seeing myself home."

"You left early."

"Go away, Mason." She turned her back on him and resumed walking.

He caught up with her. "Why'd you leave?"

"Maybe because you didn't." Oh, that was cruel. She was better than that. She didn't want to lash out at him. She just wanted some peace.

"Who is he to you?"

So that was it. His ego was bruised. "A friend."

"Not just a friend. I get the feeling it's more than that."

"It's none of your business, Mason."

"I say it is."

She stopped and shook her head, looking into his troubled eyes. It hurt to still feel something for him, to care that he was as frustrated as she was. "You can't have it both ways."

He looked puzzled. "Is that what I'm doing?"

"I have no idea what you're doing. It doesn't matter anymore. Once the fund-raiser is over, I'll be leaving, as you already mentioned."

She pivoted and continued walking. She'd gotten as far as three steps when he looped his arm around her waist, stopping her. He stood behind her, his body inches from hers, his breath at the nape of her neck, and for a minute she allowed herself to remember him, his touch, his kiss, the way he could make her feel unglued, yet whole at the same time. It wasn't to be. She had to accept it. She untangled herself from his grasp and turned to stare at him.

His arms dropped to his sides, a defeated look on his face. "Drea."

"I know you still love Larissa. I know you can't commit, so why don't we just move on and not torture ourselves this way?"

"Are you moving on with the doctor?"

She rolled her eyes. Then a fissure of anger opened up quickly becoming one giant sinkhole of incensed emotion. "No. I'm not, but not because Brad isn't wonderful. I just can't get involved with him again. I did that last time after you scarred me with your brutal rejection. I ran into the arms of the first man who'd have me. It was Brad. I shamelessly seduced him the first week of college and gave him my virginity. I gave him what I'd wanted to give you. I gave him my body, because you didn't want me and because I'd been unwanted since my mother died. And weeks later, when I turned up pregnant, the clichéd virgin too stupid to use protection, Brad was there for me. He loved me and offered to marry me."

Mason's throat was working, as though he was taking a big gulp. He stood there in stony silence.

"I almost went through with it, almost married him. But then I lost the baby, Mason. I lost my child and I was devastated. I broke up with Brad. I couldn't marry a man I didn't love. I hurt him badly, when all he wanted to do was take care of me. But you see, I couldn't love Brad. Not when I was still in love with you."

"Drea, I didn't know. I'm sorry." And she believed he was truly sorry—the emotion in his eyes was inescapable. "I never wanted to hurt you. Ever. You have to believe that."

Mason reached for her. Trembling, she moved out of his grasp, her heart breaking again. Yet it felt good to finally get the truth out, to lighten her heavy load.

"I loved you, even though I hated you, too. It doesn't make any sense, but it's true. I've never stopped loving you, Mason Boone. And all I want from you now is to leave me alone. Please. Let's get through the weekend, do our jobs, honor the people we've loved the most and then be done with it. Can you do that for me, Mason? Can you leave me alone?"

Mason's eyes grew wide; she could almost swear he was tearing up. His expression was raw, full of sympathy.

He reached out for her again and once again she backed away. She didn't want to be his friend. She didn't want to see him after this weekend. It was too hard.

"Please."

Mason finally relented, giving the smallest nod of agreement.

This time when Drea walked away, he didn't follow.

But she knew that Mason was probably still standing there, unable to move. Unable to register all that she'd confessed. She'd shocked him and worried him and made him ache with the pain he'd put her through. He probably thought she hated him again.

But that wasn't true.

She couldn't hate him.

She would probably go to her grave loving him.

Mason woke with an intense headache. He'd drunk half a bottle of bourbon last night, but even with all that mind-numbing alcohol, he couldn't forget the pain on Drea's face, the words spoken straight from her heart.

He couldn't believe what she'd gone through at seventeen years of age. He'd been responsible for that. He knew that now. He thought he'd been doing right by her by turning her away, but the honest truth was he should've never let his fascination with the olive-skinned beauty mar his judgment. He'd known she was a mixed-up kid, missing her mother, having to deal with an alcoholic father. If Mason hadn't gotten involved with her in the first place, none of it would've happened.

He pushed his hand through his hair. Just thinking about how alone Drea must've felt when she'd learned of her pregnancy, how scared she must've been, filled him with guilt. And then to lose her child…well, he knew something about that. The pain never really went away. It lingered under the surface and every time you saw a child on the street, whether laughing or crying, happy or sad, you wondered. What would your child be like had he or she lived?

It deadened a part of you and you hurt quietly, without anyone ever knowing.

A sudden knock at his door sounded more like a fire alarm going off. "What?"

"It's Aunt Lottie, Mason. Are you all right? We thought you'd be down by now."

"Who's we?" he asked, trying to sort through the cobwebs in his head.

"Larissa's parents are here."

"Holy hell." He jolted up from the bed. What time was it?

Within ten minutes, he was showered and dressed, his head still hurting like a son of a bitch as he walked into the parlor to greet his in-laws. He was in a fog, but there was one thing he was crystal-clear about this morning.

Drea had said she loved him.

And he couldn't get that out of his head.

"Paul and Wendy, good to see you." Mason shook hands with Paul Landon and then gave Wendy an embrace. She was a petite woman, much smaller than Larissa had been, but her hug was fierce and affectionate. He hugged her back with equal intensity. They'd all been through hell, and that tended to bring people closer.

They drank coffee and ate pastries, catching up on news. The Landons would stay in town for the all-important fund-raiser, which started tonight with the HeART auction.

Mason had a thousand things to oversee today, but this morning was reserved for Larissa and her parents. The time had finally come for him to drive them all to the site of Larissa's grave.

Mason visited monthly, taking a bouquet of flowers for his wife and unborn child. He grieved silently, and today, on the anniversary of Larissa's death, he'd grieve along with her parents.

They paid their respects on grounds that were impeccably groomed. It was a serene resting place. There were wrought-iron-and-wood benches under old mesquite trees; bold, beautiful statues; water stations and two chapels on the property. Mason had donated the benches; Larissa's name was engraved on the one closest to her grave.

They all stood together, laying down flowers, saying prayers, and then he walked away to give the Landons a bit of privacy.

A short time later, he felt a hand on his arm and turned to find Wendy's soft, caring eyes on him. "Mason, this is a hard day for you."

He nodded. "For you, too."

"Yes, it is. But what you're doing this weekend is a good thing. It's something that will make a difference. Paul and I feel that it takes some of the pain away. I think it's time to move forward, hard as it is. Building a cardiac wing at the hospital is a great testament to Larissa's memory. And to so many others. We can't look back anymore, Mason. We have to look ahead."

He nodded, though he felt pulled in two directions. He'd clung to his grief for so long, he almost didn't know himself without it.

"You should give yourself a break. You've mourned a long time. Maybe it's time to start a new life," she said. "Guilt-free. You deserve that, Mason. No one has honored a love more than you have."

"Thank you, Wendy."

She slipped an envelope into his hand. He thought it was a donation for the fund-raiser until he recognized the handwriting as Larissa's. "What's this?"

"I don't know. It's sealed. But when Larissa was sick she gave it to me, trusting me to give it to you. She said specifically to give it to you in two years."

Two years? "You've had it all this time."

She nodded. "It was her wish."

"Okay, thank you," he said, not knowing what to

make of it. But he wouldn't open the letter now. No, he needed privacy…and *courage*. It had taken him an entire year before he could dream about her at night without breaking down, eighteen months before he could watch videos of the two of them together. But to read words written by her when she'd been alive… That would require something he didn't know he had. Just holding the letter in his hand unsettled him. He slipped it into his jacket pocket.

Wendy seemed to understand his need to read it alone, to keep this last moment between them private.

An hour later, with the Landons promising to return this evening for the auction, Mason climbed the steps of his home. But he turned when he heard Drea's sweet laughter. She was walking with Sean Manfred, and they were obviously enjoying each other's company.

After the way they'd left off last night, he didn't think she'd want to see him. But the sound of her voice beckoned him and he turned and walked toward them.

"Hey, Mason." Sean's tone was friendly. "We were just going over the plans for the concert and dance tomorrow. The stage looks great. Drea's got everything under control."

"She always does," Mason said, meaning it.

Drea didn't hesitate to smile, and that smile reached down deep and battered the heck out of him. Apparently, she was still the grown-up of the two of them, forging ahead for the sake of the event.

"Thank you. I think we're all set for the art auction

tonight. The tent is up and the committee is busting their buns to have everything in place. The art has all come in, and it's impressive."

"Can't wait to see it," Mason told Drea.

"It's just a precursor to tomorrow. That's our big, big day," she stated, more to Sean than to him. "We have a dozen wheels turning, and hopefully, there will be no glitches. I'm happy to say the tickets for both the Fun Day and the Dinner-Dance and Dream Date are sold out. Thanks to you, Sean. I think all the high school girls in three counties bought up every raffle ticket."

"Somebody save me," he joked, his eyes wide.

"Not to fear, your date will be chaperoned."

"By you?" he asked in a hopeful tone of voice.

"No, sorry. I'll be gone by then. But I promise you'll have a good time."

"Are you leaving right after the event?" Sean asked. Mason wanted to know, too.

"My flight leaves on Sunday night."

Mason's throat tightened up. His chest hurt like hell.

"Hey, Drea, can I have a word with you?" It was Brad Williamson. He'd walked up from the festival area, his eyes only on Drea. Mason clenched his teeth. Sure, he'd tied one on last night, but his sour stomach had nothing to do with bourbon right now. Why wouldn't wonderful Brad Williamson, the guy who'd loved Drea and probably still did, get lost?

"Hi, Brad," Drea said. "I didn't expect to see you until tonight."

He scratched his head, looking too conveniently

perplexed. "Lottie had a good idea, something that would help the cause, and I wanted to run it by you."

"What is it?"

"I could give away free signed copies of my book during the festival tomorrow, if you can squeeze me in at the last minute. I have author copies I'd like to donate."

Drea's face lit up. "That's a great idea. Excuse us a minute," she said, looking at Sean.

She walked off with Brad, practically rubbing shoulders with the guy.

Sean watched her go. "She's really amazing," he said to Mason. The kid had a bad case of hero worship.

Mason nodded. "Yeah."

"Are you two…a couple?"

Mason looked at Sean. "No, we're not a couple. Why do you ask?"

He shrugged. "Back in LA, I thought you were. You seemed kinda flawless together."

Flawless… That word struck him. They *had* been flawless together, two parts of a whole. But that was back at the beach, when everything seemed surreal.

"We just work well together." Mason said, feeling the lie down to his snakeskin boots.

"Yeah… I guess," Sean said.

He wasn't sure the kid believed him.

He wasn't sure of anything anymore.

Ten

Standing inside Katie's Kupcakes' decorating booth, Drea nibbled at the raspberry cream cheese frosting, then took a giant bite of Katie's signature cupcake. "Mmm, this is the best, my friend." She licked frosting off her finger and dabbed at her mouth with a napkin. "You have outdone yourself."

Katie shook her head, her eyes bright. "You're the one who's outdone herself. Look around. This was your brainchild. Whatever money is raised, you're the one behind it."

"I had help. The volunteers have really come through," she said, thinking about Mason and how on board he'd been from the get-go. He'd been instrumental in donating his property, his time and his support to get this project off the ground in a month.

She was putting on a good show for everyone, hoping to keep the spirit of the event alive, while inside, her heart was broken. Totally, sadly broken. Tomorrow afternoon would be here before she knew it and she'd be leaving behind people she loved. Her father, her friends and…Mason. Her pain was very real, very frustrating.

The festival was in full swing and she was thankful to see the vendors' booths crowded with paying customers. Almost all the businesses in town had either made donations or offered to sell their goods at no cost to raise money for the cause. Children were taking pony rides, food and beverages were being sold, and pretty soon Katie would be swamped with young cupcake makers.

Last night's auction had been successful. Every item had been purchased. Drea wouldn't know the final weekend tally for some time, but all in all, things were going smoothly.

Her father walked up and kissed her cheek, wrapping his arm around her waist. "Hi, sweetheart," he said.

"Hi, Daddy. Glad you made it out today."

"You're looking good, Mr. M," Katie said. "Want a cupcake?"

"Ah, thank you, Katie. But actually, I came to see if I can help you girls today."

Katie glanced at Drea and then back at him. "Sure. I could use a hand in here. Gonna need to keep the cupcakes and frosting flowing when the booth opens for decorating."

"Glad to help," he said.

Drea and her father had come to terms with the past, and ever since then, their relationship had flourished. He was back to being her dad, the man she'd known before her mother died, the man who was a loving father and sound businessman. She'd have days and days in New York to get over it, but now was a time for healing between them. She wanted to leave on a good note.

She glanced across the field to where Brad was setting up his booth. Luckily, they'd had extra room for him. "If you two have it covered, I need to check on something."

Katie gave her a nod. "Go. Your dad and I will handle the kids."

"Thanks. I won't be long."

Drea walked through the crowds of people having a great time. When she arrived at Brad's booth, she said hello.

"Hi, yourself, pretty lady. This festival is really something."

"It is. Thanks. And thanks for donating your time and books. There are a lot of families here, and I'm sure many parents are in need of advice about their toddlers."

"Uh, Drea? May I have a word with you?"

"Of course," she said, curious about what Brad wanted to discuss.

He took her hand and walked her to the back of the booth. "I know you're leaving tomorrow, and I'll be back in New York in a month. I was wondering if you…and me. Well, if I can call you sometime."

Drea paused, trying to hide her indecision, and not

doing a very good job, judging by the wary expression on Brad's face.

"We've been through a lot together, Drea. I know there's painful history between us, but I care very much about you. I never stopped."

If he had anything but friendship in mind, she'd have to come clean. She didn't want to use Brad, to run to him just because things got rough and lonely when she got back home. And she didn't want to hurt him again.

"I know you do. And I care very much about you," she said, as sincerely as she knew how. "But the truth is, I'm in love with someone."

Brad let a beat go by. "It's Mason, isn't it?"

She gave him a long look and nodded. "Is it that obvious?"

Brad smiled. "Ever since you walked over here, Mason's had his eyes on you. He's like a hawk, that guy. And I think he'd like to kill me where I stand for talking to you."

She rolled her eyes. "Please."

They laughed, but when she turned around she found Mason's deep, smoky eyes on her, and her heart skittered to a halt. He was leaning against a tree, his hat tipped low, cowboy-style, his jeans and black boots dusty. He'd been helping out with the ponies making sure the riders were safely on their mounts.

It wasn't fair that he had the ability to turn her life upside down like this. Their eyes connected for a moment and it was as if his heat traveled across the twenty feet of space between them. He was all she saw through the crowd and her insides immediately warmed up.

She dropped her head and sighed. "It's impossible." Then she brushed a chaste kiss on Brad's cheek. "I'd better go. Good luck today. I'll be sure to talk to you later."

Drea walked away, getting as far from Mason as possible, heading toward the Boone kitchen, where the caterers were prepping for tonight's dinner and dance.

Hours later, the sun set in a brilliant orange blaze. All the festival goers who'd filled up on fun, cupcakes, rides and games, were gone. On another part of the grounds, a stage was ready for The Band Blue. Fifty round tables with elegant white tablecloths and short pillar candles surrounded the parquet dance floor.

People were arriving for the dinner and concert. Women were dressed in classic Western wear, jean skirts and leather boots or elegant gowns or somewhere in between. Drea, being the co-master of ceremonies had put her best foot forward, treating herself to a form-fitting gold gown. Shimmering sequins covered the crisscross back straps. Her hair was held away from her face with two rhinestone clips, allowing it to flow softly down her back.

Mason walked up behind her, putting a hand on her shoulder. "Are you ready for this?"

She glanced at him, felt his familiar mind-numbing touch, and for a moment her breath stuck in her throat. He wore his suit well, a dark three-piece with a gold brocade vest. In another lifetime she would've grabbed him by his bolo tie and dragged him behind the stage to have her way with him.

What a dream that would be. "I think so."

He leaned in close and whispered, "You look like a goddess."

"Th-thank you." She absorbed the compliment and they stood there together, in the background, watching the donors taking their seats.

When everything was in place, Mason took her hand. "Let's do this," he said.

They walked up on the stage together. Mason gave her the floor first. She went to the podium and spoke from the heart, thanking everyone for coming, thanking all the volunteers and thanking The Band Blue for donating their time. "This is a project near and dear to so many of us, but as you know, both my family and the Boones have lost someone to heart disease. We hope, with all of your generous donations, we will make our ambitious goal of raising two million dollars for the cardiac wing. I hear we've come close, as donations have been pouring in from citizens who couldn't attend the festivities this weekend." Drea put her fist over her heart, tears welling in her eyes. "This means so much to me, personally. Thank you all."

She turned to find Mason's eyes on her, filled with pride. There was a moment between them, something sacred, something that went beyond their personal relationship issues, something that connected them. Nothing could ever take that away. "And now Mason Boone will say a few words."

As he sidled up to the podium she began to walk

away, but he discreetly curled his hand around her waist, drawing her close. They stood beside each other, and Mason took over the microphone. "Once again let me thank everyone who helped put this fund-raiser together. All of you have done a great job and we can't thank you enough. I have to give most of the credit to the woman standing beside me, Andrea MacDonald. She has been absolutely dedicated to the cause.

"Our goal was to break ground on the new wing in two years, but the Boone family hopes to make that a reality even sooner. To that end, our family is pledging an additional one million dollars to the cause."

Applause broke out. Drea opened her mouth to speak, but words wouldn't come. She stared at Mason as he continued. "The only stipulation I have is to be able to name the new cardiac wing. It will be called the Maria MacDonald Heart Center."

He turned to Drea then, his dark eyes full of emotion, and she'd never loved him more.

"Th-thank you," she mouthed, still unable to speak aloud.

"And there'll be a garden on the grounds named for my late wife. It'll be called Larissa's Blooms."

Mason paused a second, struggling a bit. Then he went on. "Miss MacDonald and I hope you have a wonderful evening, starting off with a concert from Grammy nominees The Band Blue. Feel free to come up onto the dance floor and swing your partner around. Oh, and after dinner, be warned, we'll be raffling off a Dream Date with Sean Manfred. You girls on the back lawn there will just have to be patient."

There were hundreds of girls sitting beyond the tables, under the twinkling lights strung from the trees. Their raffle tickets had also admitted them to the concert.

Drea and Mason walked off the stage just as the band stepped up to take their places.

Her mind swirling, she heard Sean give the guests a warm welcome. But just as she turned to speak to Mason about his generosity, a local news reporter with a film crew nabbed him.

"Mr. Boone, do you have time for that interview now?"

Mason sighed. "Sure thing. Give me one second, okay?"

Of course they'd want to speak with Mason. After his announcement and personal donation to the cause, he was newsworthy.

He looked into her eyes. "Save some time for me later. Maybe a dance?"

She didn't want to dance with him. She didn't want to suffer any more than necessary. Her scars were too raw right now. Mason had impacted her life in too many ways to name, and she would never forget him. But the sad fact remained, that he'd had many opportunities this month to sort out his feelings for her. To allow himself a fresh start and get over his guilt and pain. To allow someone else in. He, too, was scarred. He, too, had endured great loss. And it was extremely hard for him. It was hard for her, as well, but at least she was willing to take the chance.

It was obvious he wasn't.

"I…c-can't, Mason. I'll always remember you and this." She spread her arms out to encompass the festival. "We did a wonderful thing here. And…well, naming the wing in my mother's honor was…"

Once again stung by his generosity, she felt her eyes begin to burn. She didn't want to cry in front of him. "Thank you." It was all she could say. "You'd better get on with that interview."

She turned away from him then and headed for her dad who was standing off to one side looking a bit overwhelmed and misty-eyed after the announcement honoring her mother Maria. He needed her as much as she needed him right now.

Her heartache aside, she and Mason pulled this weekend off, and with the Boone's charitable donation, they may have far exceeded their goals. She had to feel good about that.

Evening turned into night as the band played, wowing the guests. Dinner was served when the band took their first break, and then as they began to play their second set, Sean encouraged everyone to get up on the dance floor.

Drea found Lottie sitting at the Boone table off to the side, and took a seat next to her. Lottie gave her a big hug. "Drea, this has been a fantastic evening. I'm so proud of what you have accomplished."

"Thanks. I'm really thrilled with the outcome."

"Thrilled?" Lottie's eyes narrowed a bit and she took both Drea's hands in hers. "I don't see thrill on your face, sweetheart. I see sadness and regret."

"I'm leaving tomorrow afternoon. I didn't think I'd say this, but I'm going to miss Boone Springs. And my dad."

Lottie stiffened at the mention of Drew. "I understand. This place is your true home, Drea. You've got roots here. And friends."

"I do. I promised Dad I'll come visit often. We're doing pretty well now and I've forgiven him for what he did. But Lottie, what's up between the two of you? I've noticed you haven't spent a minute together this entire weekend."

"Oh, um…" Lottie shook her head and glanced away. "I'm afraid he's very angry with me. He's been avoiding me for days. You know us. We've always had a rocky relationship."

"Yes, but…I thought this time things were different."

They were interrupted by the sound of Mason's voice coming from the microphone onstage. "And now it's time to announce the winner of the Dream Date with Sean raffle. To do the honors, our own publicity pro, Linda Sullivan, will come up here and pull the winning ticket. As you know, Linda was instrumental in putting this part of the event together."

When Linda reached the stage, Mason turned the mic over to her. She made a few jokes about the girls languishing on the back lawn, waiting for this moment. Then she had Sean come up to a big Plexiglass cube filled with raffle tickets. "It's only fitting that Sean pick the winner. Don't you think so, girls?"

Shouts and giddy laughter broke out as Linda gestured for Sean to dig deep into the cube and grab a ticket. Everyone at the tables and on the lawn quieted.

"And the dream date with Sean goes to…Regina Clayborne!"

Lofty sighs of disappointment filled the back lawn, except for where the winner was standing, surrounded by her friends. She began jumping for joy, her blond hair bouncing in the breeze. Linda brought her up onstage to meet Sean and the girl couldn't stop crying happy tears.

"Well, I guess my part is officially over," Drea said to Lottie. "I think the committee can finish up tomorrow."

"What are your plans then?"

"I want to spend the entire morning with my father. My flight leaves in the late afternoon."

Lottie folded her arms around her middle, looking none too pleased. "And here I was hoping that you and Mason would have worked it out by now."

"I can't fight a ghost, Lottie. I can't make Mason feel things he doesn't."

"You're hurting."

"Love hurts sometimes."

Lottie's eyes glistened with moisture. "Yeah, sweetheart, sometimes it does."

As the guests filed out of the concert area and the band packed up to go back to their hotel, Mason walked over to the Boone family table and found Lottie sitting with Risk and Lucas.

"Well done, brother," Risk said.

Luke nodded in agreement.

"Thanks, guys." Mason should be flying high. After this past month of hard work, their fund-raiser had achieved its goals. The new cardiac wing of the hospital was destined to break ground, but one important thing was missing. Or one person, rather. "Didn't I see Drea sitting here a few minutes ago?"

"You did," Luke said. "But she's gone now. I grabbed a dance with her earlier this evening."

"Yeah. Me, too," Risk said. "She's pretty light on her feet."

Mason gave his brothers a good-natured frown. They liked busting his chops. "So where did she go?"

"Home, I think," Lottie said.

Mason swallowed hard. "Already?"

"She said she was tired and had some packing to do."

Risk sipped from his glass of wine. "She promised to come back to Boone Springs soon, though. I made a date to take her to dinner."

"Yeah. Me, too," Lucas added.

"All right, boys," Aunt Lottie said to Mason's pain-in-the-ass brothers. "You've made your point. Let me have a chat with Mason."

The guys got up, and both gave him a conciliatory pat on the back before walking off.

"Mason, what's going on?" Aunt Lottie asked.

He slumped into the seat next to her. "I just need to talk to Drea."

"No, you don't. The time for talking is over between you two. You have to act. And if you can't, then it's best you leave that girl alone."

"Are you saying I've been taking advantage of her, Aunt Lottie?"

"That's not what I'm saying, my thickheaded nephew. What I am saying is that you have less than twenty-four hours to figure out what you truly want. If it's not her, then let her leave town. And you should resume your life."

Resume his dreary life? Go back to all that emptiness? Go back to dwelling on his loss, dwelling on the pain? Go back to life before Drea? What in hell was wrong with him? He couldn't do that.

Aunt Lottie was right.

He needed to act.

Wearing daisy-yellow gardening gloves, Drea inserted the last vinca plant in the landscaped border surrounding the cottage and then gave the soil a loving pat. The garden was finished, returned to its former glory. That had been her goal.

Her father watched from the front porch. "Drea, don't you tire yourself out now."

"I'm not. It feels good to finish this. Doesn't it look great?" She stood up to gaze at her handiwork. Flowers and shrubs adorned the land once overrun by weeds.

Drew came down the steps, his eyes sharper than she'd seen them in a long time. "Yeah, it's beautiful."

"You have to promise to keep the weeds at bay and water the plants."

"After all your hard work, you know I will." He looked at his watch. She had only a few hours left at home with him.

"You ready for breakfast now, sweetheart? I made you pancakes with chocolate chips and apple bacon and—"

"Whoa, Dad. You had me at chocolate chip pancakes."

He laughed and hugged her shoulders. "Go shower and I'll get the meal on the table."

She kissed his cheek. "You're on."

Half an hour later, Drea patted her stomach and pushed her plate away. She'd dressed in the clothes she'd wear later when she boarded her plane, a soft pink, lightweight sweater and a pair of designer jeans that were feeling a little snug about now. "I ate too much."

Her dad grinned. "Me, too. How about we take a little walk, burn off some of those pancakes."

Whatever he wanted to do, she was game. This was their last morning together for a while and she was happy just being with him. Walking in the morning air would help keep her mind off leaving town. "That's a great idea."

"I'm ready." Her father glanced at his watch again. "Let's go."

They walked down the road a bit, taking sure but slow steps, just enjoying the scenery and weather this autumn morning. Drew MacDonald was healthier than when she'd come. He'd been eating better and had lost some weight, and his daily walking rituals were really helping build his strength.

About a quarter mile into the walk, after rounding a turn, she spotted a black SUV parked on the side of the road just a few feet away. A man climbed out, long

legs in fitted black jeans, silver belt buckle gleaming, with a familiar Stetson atop his head. Mason.
Her heart began to pound. "Dad, what's going on?"

Her father's eyes grew soft and he smiled. "Hear
him out, darlin' girl."

"What?"

"Mason needs to speak with you."

Her mind clicked away. "But I don't want… Is
this a trap?"

Her father grinned. "God, I hope so." He kissed
her cheek and gave her a big hug. "Don't be mad, and
listen to your heart." With that, he turned around and
began walking back toward the cottage, leaving her
dumbfounded in the middle of the road.

It took only four long strides for Mason to reach
her. He gave her a warm smile, as if he hadn't just
hijacked her. "Mornin'."

She clamped her mouth closed. She didn't like surprises. At least not like this, especially when Mason
was looking all casual and gorgeous. But his eyes,
those dark, dark eyes, weren't filled with his usual
confidence. He had that vulnerable look on his face
that always got to her.

"Good to see you." His gaze flowed over her in-
tently as if…as if he was… No. She wasn't going to
think it. She wasn't going to hope. Mason had made
his choice and it wasn't her.

"What's this all about, Mason?"

"It's about me and you. I want to show you something."

"I don't think so. I'm supposed to—"

"Please," he said. "It won't take long and I'll bring you back to Drew's quickly." He extended his hand, palm up, and waited.

She gestured to the car. "Are you driving me somewhere?"

"That's the plan. It's not far."

Listen to your heart. Listen to your heart. Her father's advice helped her make the choice.

She began slowly walking to the SUV, ignoring Mason's outstretched hand. She wasn't going to make this easy on him, whatever it was. But her reluctance didn't faze him. Instead, he raced to open the car door for her and she climbed in.

Mason got in and didn't look at her, didn't say anything. They drove in silence down the road and then Mason took a cutoff that led to the west end of the property that was once Thundering Hills.

He stopped the car and they both got out, her heart hammering in her chest. At one time, this had been MacDonald land, her home. She hadn't come here in a long, long time.

Mason leaned against the grill of his car and grabbed her hand so she landed next to him.

"Sean said something to me the other day that made a lot of sense," he said softly, his eyes touching hers. "He said you and I were flawless together."

She blinked. "Sean said that?"

"Yeah. The kid's pretty damn smart."

"Unlike you."

He laughed and it was so hearty, she had to smile, too. "When you're right, you're right."

"Excuse me, did I hear correctly?"

"You did. You heard me right. And I got to think-ing that when we were first together, some weeks back, I thought you were good for me. There was something about you that jump-started my life again. You were the catalyst I needed, the fire under my ass, whatever you want to call it. I don't know, maybe it was because we had history together, but you came to Rising Springs and saved me from drowning in my own grief. After that one kiss, I was suddenly filled with light and energy and I wanted more. I wanted to feel again. But I was afraid, too, because I'd clung to Larissa's memory for so long and I didn't know if I could go through something like that again. I didn't know if my emotions were all screwed up."

"What are you saying, Mason?"

"I'm saying that after I learned about what hap-pened to you in college, I freaked out a little bit. I blamed myself for getting involved with you, for tak-ing advantage of a much younger woman."

"But you didn't. I wanted you, Mason. It was your rejection that hurt me. I wasn't a very secure girl back then, and I guess I understand now why you did what you did."

He squeezed her hands and looked solemnly into her eyes. "We've both been hurt in the past, and it's time to put that behind us, Drea. Sweetheart, I realize now that all those sparks you ignited in me weren't just sexual. It was love, Drea. I love you. You're the only woman for me. We are meant for each other and I can't stand the thought of you leaving. We belong together."

It was a stunning declaration that left her breathless. But she wasn't sure she could truly trust it. "Mason, are you sure you're ready? I know you care about me, but love?"

"Believe me when I say I am ready. Granted, I'm a late bloomer, but last night, after you left the event, it finally hit me how much I love you. I'm never afraid when I'm with you, Drea. Just the opposite. When I'm with you, I am the man I'm supposed to be. I was so sure of myself last night at our event that I asked your father for his blessing, and he gave it to me. Drea, I want to do it again, I want to marry you. I want a family with as many kids as you'd like. I want it all, as long as it's with you."

She smiled at the notion. It was a precious thought. She wanted babies with Mason. Lots and lots of them. All week long, she'd been dreading going back to New York, dreading leaving this place that now felt so much like home, her true home. In her heart of hearts, here with Mason was where she really wanted to be.

Mason got down on one knee and presented her with a brilliant square-cut diamond ring. It was so beautiful her breath caught in a big gasp.

"Andrea MacDonald, I promise to love and honor you for the rest of our lives. Will you marry me?"

She took his upturned face in her hands, gazing into those dark, sincere, beautiful eyes. "Yes, Mason. My dream, my heart. I'll marry you."

He grinned widely and placed the ring on her finger. "My grandmother would have been happy to see her ring on your finger, Drea. She would've welcomed you and loved you almost as much as I do."

He stood then and claimed her lips in a kiss that sealed their love. A kiss that meant forever. And they stayed cradled in each other's arms for long, sweet moments, Mason stroking her hair as she gazed out onto the hills.

"When you brought me out here, you said you wanted to show me something?" she finally asked, looking at him curiously.

"I wanted to propose to you here, on the land you've always loved. We can build a place of our own here, if you'd like. We can design a house you'll love overlooking the hills."

"I'd like that. I guess I'm moving back to Rising Springs."

Mason pulled away slightly. "I know your career is important to you and I'll support whatever you want to do about it. You don't have to decide now, sweetheart."

Her job had once been the only thing she'd actually had in her life. And since coming home, she realized that there was so much more she wanted. She loved Boone Springs. She loved her father and her friends. And she loved Mason Boone, more than she'd thought possible. "Actually, I think I'd like to do volunteer work in Boone Springs. I can donate my time and hope to continue to make a difference here."

"That sounds like a good plan."

"It's the best plan as long as we're together," she said.

"It is," he agreed, placing a light kiss on her forehead. "Missy isn't selling the beach house, after all.

She decided to keep it for family and friends. And I was thinking it's a good place for our honeymoon. Shall I book it, say, for the spring?"

"You want to get married that quickly?" Drea asked, liking the idea of being Mason's wife.

"I do. As soon as we can plan the wedding."

She leaned against him, looking out at the place she'd once called home, the place she would finally return to. It was uncanny, something she never would have believed possible.

"And there's one more thing," he said quietly. "Larissa's parents gave me a letter she wrote to me two years ago, right before she passed. It's her last words to me. I haven't opened it yet."

"Why not?"

Mason drew a deep breath and pulled an envelope out of his pocket. "I didn't realize the reason I've been holding on to this letter until last night. It's because I wanted you by my side when I read it. Larissa was my past, and I loved her deeply, but you…you are my future. And I needed you to know that no matter what's inside this letter, it won't change my love for you. You need to know how much I love you."

"I think I do now," she said, her eyes filling with tears. "I love you very much, Mason. If you're ready, go ahead, read the letter privately." She squeezed his forearm, holding on to him. "I'm right here and I always will be."

Mason unsealed the envelope and pulled out the piece of paper. He took a few moments to read Larissa's words and then faced Drea. He swallowed hard, his eyes glistening. "Larissa knew me so well. She knew I'd grieve a long time. She said she wanted me to be happy, to find someone to share my life with. She wanted me to move on."

He sighed and then kissed Drea's lips gently, sweetly, and she felt his love all the way down to her toes. "And I have, Drea. I am moving on. I've found happiness with you. I promise you'll never doubt my love. We'll have a good life."

"Yes we will, Mason. I believe it, too. After all, together the two of us are absolutely *flawless*."

* * * * *

If you loved Mason and Drea,
you won't want to miss
Risk Boone's story
by USA TODAY *bestselling author*
Charlene Sands.

Available September 2019
exclusively from Harlequin Desire!

COMING NEXT MONTH FROM

HARLEQUIN® *Desire*

Available June 4, 2019

#2665 HIS TO CLAIM
The Westmoreland Legacy • by Brenda Jackson
Honorary Westmoreland Thurston "Mac" McRoy delayed a romantic ranch vacation with his wife for too long—she went without him! Now it will take all his skills to rekindle their desire and win back his wife...

#2666 RANCHER IN HER BED
Texas Cattleman's Club: Houston • by Joanne Rock
Rich rancher Xander Currin isn't looking for a relationship. Cowgirl Frankie Walsh won't settle for anything less. When combustible desire consumes them both just as secrets from Frankie's past come to light, will their passion survive?

#2667 TAKEN BY STORM
Dynasties: Secrets of the A-List • by Cat Schield
Isabel Withers knows her boss, hotel executive Shane Adams, should be off-limits—but the chances he'll notice her are zilch. Until they're stranded together in a storm and let passion rule. Can their forbidden love overcome the scandals waiting for them?

#2668 THE BILLIONAIRE'S BARGAIN
Blackout Billionaires • by Naima Simone
Chicago billionaire Darius King never surrenders...until a blackout traps him with an irresistible beauty. Then the light reveals his enemy—his late best friend's widow! Marriage is the only way to protect his friend's legacy, but soon her secrets will force Darius to question everything...

#2669 FROM MISTAKE TO MILLIONS
Switched! • by Andrea Laurence
A DNA kit just proved Jade Nolan is *not* a Nolan. Desperate for answers, she accepts the help of old flame Harley Dalton—even though she knows she can't resist him. What will happen when temptation leads to passion and the truth complicates everything?

#2670 STAR-CROSSED SCANDAL
Plunder Cove • by Kimberley Troutte
When Chloe Harper left Hollywood to reunite with her family, she vowed to heal herself before hooking up with *anyone*. But now sexy star-maker Nicolas Medeiros is at her resort, offering her the night of her dreams. She takes it...and more. But how will she let him go?

YOU CAN FIND MORE INFORMATION ON UPCOMING HARLEQUIN® TITLES, FREE EXCERPTS AND MORE AT WWW.HARLEQUIN.COM.

HDCNM0519

It was her first kiss. But that didn't matter.

It was Dane. That was all that mattered. That was all that really mattered.

Dane, the man she'd fantasized about a hundred times—maybe a thousand times—doing this very thing. But this was so much brighter and more vivid than a fantasy could ever be. Color and texture and taste. The rough whiskers on his face, the heat of his breath, the way those big, sure hands cupped her face as his lips moved slowly over hers.

She took a step and the shattered glass crunched beneath her feet, but she didn't care. She didn't care at all. She wanted to breathe in this moment for as long as she could, broken glass be damned. To exist just like this, with his lips against hers, for as long as she possibly could.

She leaned forward, wrapped her fingers around the fabric of his T-shirt and clung to him, holding them both steady, because she was afraid she might fall if she didn't.

Her knees were weak. Like in a book or a movie.

She hadn't known that kissing could really, literally, make your knees weak. Or that touching a man you wanted could make you feel like you were burning up, like you had a fever. Could make you feel hollow and restless and desperate for what came next…

Even if what came next scared her a little.

It was Dane.

She trusted Dane.

With her secrets. With her body.

Dane.

She breathed his name on a whispered sigh as she moved to take their kiss deeper, and found herself being set back, glass crunching beneath her feet yet again.

"I should go," he said, his voice rough.

"No!" The denial burst out of her, and she found herself reaching forward to grab his shirt again. "No," she said again, this time a little less crazy and desperate.

She didn't feel any less crazy and desperate.

"I have to go, Bea."

"You don't. You could stay."

The look he gave her burned her down to the soles of her feet. "I can't."

"If you're worried about… I didn't misunderstand. I mean I know that if you stayed we would…"

"Dammit, Bea," he bit out. "We can't. You know that."

"Why? I'm not stupid. I know you don't want… I don't want…" She stumbled over her words because it all seemed stupid. To say something as inane as she knew they wouldn't get married. Even saying it made her feel like a silly virgin.

She was a virgin. There wasn't really any glossing over that. But she didn't have to seem silly.

She did know, though. For all that everyone saw her as soft and naive, she wasn't. She'd carried a torch for Dane for a long time but she'd also realistically seen how marriage worked. Her brother was a cheater. Her mother was a cheater.

Her father was… She didn't even know.

That was the legacy of love and marriage in her family.

Truly, she didn't want any part of it.

Some companionship, though. Sex. She wanted that. With him. Why couldn't she have that? McKenna made it sound simple, and possible. And Bea wanted it.

Don't miss
Unbroken Cowboy *by Maisey Yates,*
available May 2019 wherever Harlequin® books
and ebooks are sold.

www.Harlequin.com

SPECIAL EXCERPT FROM

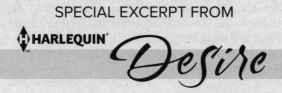
HARLEQUIN Desire

*Honorary Westmoreland Thurston "Mac" McRoy
delayed a romantic ranch vacation with his wife for too
long—she went without him! Now it will take all his
skills to rekindle their desire and win back his wife…*

Read on for a sneak peek at
His to Claim
by New York Times *bestselling author Brenda Jackson!*

Thurston McRoy, called Mac by all who knew him, still had
his arms around his mother's shoulders when he felt her tense
up. "Mom? You okay?" he asked, looking down at her.

When his parents glanced over at each other, that uneasy
feeling from earlier crept over him again. Not liking it, he
turned to go down the hall toward his bedroom when his father
reached out to stop him.

"Teri isn't here, Mac."

Mac turned back to his father. His mother had moved to
stand beside his dad.

"It's after two in the morning and tomorrow is a school day
for the girls. So where is she?"

His mother reached out and touched his arm. "She needed
to get away and she asked if we would come keep the girls."

Mac frowned. He knew his wife. She would not have gone
anywhere without their daughters. "What do you mean, she
needed to get away? Why?"

"She's the one who has to tell you that, Thurston. It's not
for us to say."

Mac drew in a deep breath, not understanding any of this. Because his parents were acting so secretive, he felt his confusion and anger escalating. "Fine. Where is she?"

It was his father who spoke. "She left three days ago for the Torchlight Dude Ranch."

Mac's frown deepened. "The Torchlight Dude Ranch? In Wyoming?"

"Yes."

"What the hell did she go there for?"

His father didn't say anything for a minute and then gave Mac an answer. "She said she always wanted to go back there."

Mac rubbed his hand across his face. Yes, Teri had always wanted to go back there, the place he'd taken her on their honeymoon, a little over ten years ago. And he'd always promised to take her back. But between his covert missions and their growing family, there had never been enough time. Teri, who'd been raised on a ranch in Texas, was a cowgirl at heart and had once dreamed of being on the rodeo circuit due to her roping and riding skills. She'd even represented the state of Texas as a rodeo queen years ago.

When they'd married, she had given it all up to travel around the world with her naval husband. She'd said she'd done so gladly. Why in the world would Teri leave their kids and go to a dude ranch by herself?

He knew the only person who could answer that question was Teri.

It was time to go find his wife.

His to Claim
by New York Times *bestselling author Brenda Jackson,
available June 2019 wherever
Harlequin® Desire books and ebooks are sold.*

www.Harlequin.com

Love Harlequin romance?

DISCOVER.

Be the first to find out about promotions,
news and exclusive content!

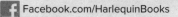 Facebook.com/HarlequinBooks

Twitter.com/HarlequinBooks

Instagram.com/HarlequinBooks

Pinterest.com/HarlequinBooks

ReaderService.com

EXPLORE.

Sign up for the Harlequin e-newsletter and
download a free book from any series at
TryHarlequin.com.

CONNECT.

Join our Harlequin community to share
your thoughts and connect with other
romance readers!
Facebook.com/groups/HarlequinConnection

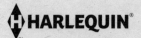 **HARLEQUIN®**

**ROMANCE WHEN
YOU NEED IT**

HSOCIAL2018

 MAY 2019